0121   KINGSTANDING
464 5193   LIBRARY

Loans are up to 28 days. Fines are charged if items are
not returned by the due date. Items can be renewed
at the Library, via the internet or by telephone up to
3 times. Items in demand will not be renewed.
Please use a bookmark

Date for return		
2 1 OCT 2014	2 2 JUL 2017	2 2 JUN 2019
2 1 FEB 2015		2 6 JUL 2019
1 9 JUN 2015	- 1 SEP 2018	
1 8 JUL 2015	- 6 NOV 2018	
2 4 AUG 2015	1 5 JAN 2019	

Check out our online catalogue to see what's in stock,
or to renew or reserve books.
www.birmingham.gov.uk/libcat
www.birmingham.bov.uk/libraries

 **Birmingham City Council**

Q45612r1

Also by Sarah Prineas

THE MAGIC THIEF
Book One

BOOK TWO

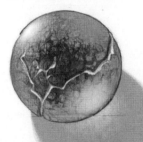

BY SARAH PRINEAS

ILLUSTRATIONS BY
ANTONIO JAVIER CAPARO

Quercus

First published in Great Britain in 2009 by
Quercus
21 Bloomsbury Square
London
WC1A 2NS

Published in America by HarperCollins Children's Books
a division of HarperCollins Publishers, Inc.
1350 Avenue of the Americas, New York 10019, USA

A CIP catalogue reference for this book is available
from the British Library

ISBN (HB) 978 1 84724 854 1
ISBN (TPB) 978 1 84724 855 8

10 9 8 7 6 5 4 3 2 1

This book printed and bound in England by
Clays Ltd, St Ives plc.

TO THEO,
BECAUSE THE BIRD
WAS HIS IDEA

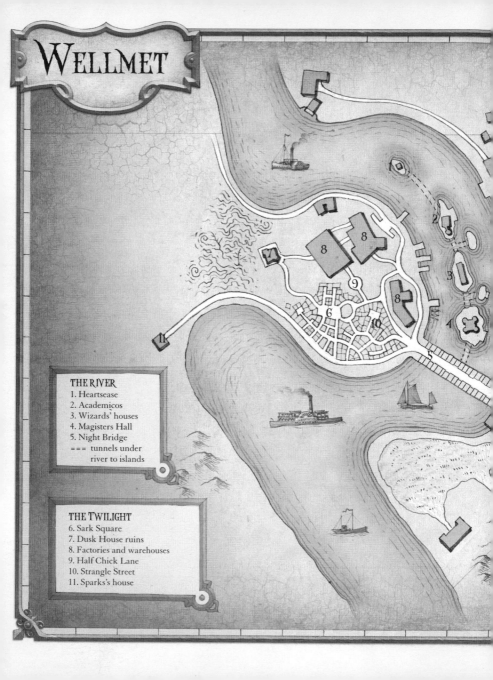

WELLMET

THE RIVER
1. Heartsease
2. Academicos
3. Wizards' houses
4. Magisters Hall
5. Night Bridge
=== tunnels under
    river to islands

THE TWILIGHT
6. Sark Square
7. Dusk House ruins
8. Factories and warehouses
9. Half Chick Lane
10. Strangle Street
11. Sparks's house

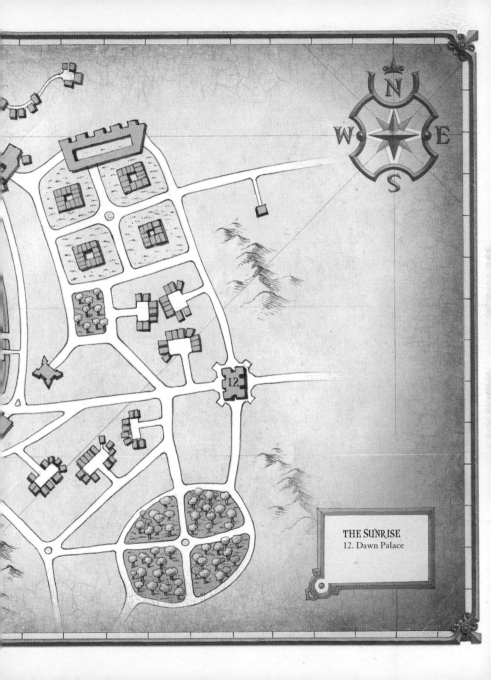

THE SUNRISE
12. Dawn Palace

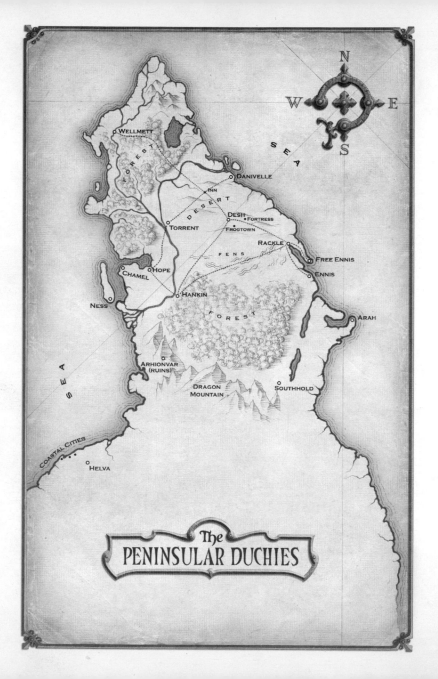

The
PENINSULAR DUCHIES

CHAPTER 1

'A wizard is a lot like a pyrotechnist,' I said.

'You mean magic and explosions, boy?' Nevery said from the doorway of my workroom. In one hand he held his gold knob-headed cane, and he had his flat-brimmed hat under his arm. He'd just gotten back from a magisters' meeting, which always made him grumpy.

'They'd be controlled explosions,' I said.

'*Controlled* explosions? That would seem to be a contradiction in terms, Connwaer.' He looked around my workroom and scowled.

Benet had helped me strip the faded wallpaper from the walls and whitewash them, and I'd swept the floor and scrubbed the grime and dust off the tall windows and set Lady, the white and tabby-tailed cat, to deal with the mice. A few books from Nevery's library were stacked neatly on the shelves. After everything was ready I'd hung my picture of a dragon, the one I'd nicked from Nevery's study, on the wall. The picture was so sooty and dirty from hanging over a fireplace that it looked like a dragon hidden behind a cloud, but I could make out a gleam of golden wing and a snakelike tail and a sharp eye, red like an ember in a hearth.

I'd been reading Prattshaw's treatise on pyro-technics. The book lay open on the table in front of me, along with some papers and a dirty teacup.

'Yes, this is a bad idea,' Nevery said. 'What would pyrotechnics accomplish, hmmm?'

That was a very good question.

To do magic, every wizard had to find his or her own special locus magicalicus. It could be a piece of gravel or a small chunk of crystal or a rounded river stone or a pebble found in the street. When you found it you knew, for it called to you. My own locus stone had been the finest jewel in the city, the centre stone from the duchess's necklace, leaf green and glowing with its own light, and it had been my way to talk to the magic. It had been destroyed when I'd freed the magic from Crowe's prisoning device. After that, I'd spent most of the summer looking all over Wellmet for another one. Nevery'd told me I'd find a new locus stone, but I hadn't. Then I checked every grimoire in the academicos, and none of them said anything about wizards finding a second locus stone. If their first stone was destroyed, they died along with it. But I hadn't died.

'Well, Nevery,' I said, 'the magic talked to me when the Underlord's device exploded.' Nobody except Nevery believed me, but I knew what I'd heard. 'If I make a very small pyrotechnic explosion, it might talk to me again.' And then I could be a wizard, even without a locus stone.

'Hmph,' Nevery said. 'Pyrotechnics is not a reliable method, boy.' He paced across the room and leaned over the table to lift the book I was reading to see the title. 'Prattshaw,' he said, dropping the book. He shook his head. 'I suppose you can't get into too much trouble just reading about it. Don't be late for supper,' he said, and swept-stepped out of my workroom and down the stairs.

Had I ever been late for supper? No.

I went back to the book. Tourmalifine and slowsilver, it said, were *contrafusives*; that meant slowsilver attracted and confined magic, and tourmalifine repelled it. When mingled, they exploded.

I closed the book and set it aside. In a box under the table where Nevery couldn't see it, I had a stoppered vial of tourmalifine crystals. And I had a little lockbox with a few drops of slowsilver in it that I'd nicked from Nevery's workroom.

I brought out the vial and the lockbox. The book said that very small amounts of slowsilver and tourmalifine caused very small explosions – just puffs of smoke, really. Clear as clear, Nevery didn't want me doing pyrotechnics. But he wouldn't notice a puff of smoke, would he?

With the raggedy sleeve of my apprentice's robe, I wiped out the teacup and set it on the table; then I tipped in a few crystals of tourmalifine, careful not to get any on my fingers. I didn't have a key for the lockbox, so I pulled out my lockpick wires, snick-picked the lock, and opened it. The slowsilver swirled at the bottom of the box. As I set the lid back, it crept up the sides, almost like it was trying to escape. I tapped the box, and the slowsilver slid back to the bottom again.

I dipped the end of one of my lockpick wires into the slowsilver. A mirror-bright bead clung to it as I lifted it out. Carefully – *steady hands* – I brought the slowsilver to the teacup and tapped it from the end of the wire. Like a drop of water landing on sand, it splatted into the centre of the little pile of tourmalifine in the bottom of the cup.

I held my breath and bent closer to see.

The slowsilver soaked into the tourmalifine. I counted *one*, *two*, *thr* –

With a *pop* the cup shattered. A whirl of fizz-green sparks flung me away from the table and fountained up to the ceiling, then swarmed round the room, crashing from wall to wall. I scrambled to my feet. On the table, the vial of tourmalifine cracked open like an egg, spilling green crystals across the tabletop; the box of slowsilver tipped over, and a silver-bright snail crept out.

'No!' I shouted, and grabbed for the slow-silver. It squirmed out of my fingers and I ducked as the sparks flew over my head again, *whoosh*.

The slowsilver reached the tourmalifine. They mingled.

In a corner of the ceiling, a whirling ball of sparks and fire gathered, then streaked across the room, knocked the table over, and slammed into me.

At the same moment, the mingled elements exploded.

I lay flat on the floor and ducked my head. White fire and crackling sparks filled the room. And so did the voice of the magic. *Damrodellodesseldesh*, it began, the words vibrating low and slow in the bones of my arms and legs. *Ellarhionvar*, it went on, faster and higher, the words rattling around in my skull. Then a shriek that made my teeth hurt, *arhionvarliardenliesh*!

Then, silence.

To the Magisters,
Magisters Hall, Wellmet.

Because you are clearly unwilling – or unable – to understand what happened when Dusk House was destroyed, I will explain it to you yet again. The explosion at Dusk House was not – I repeat, not – a pyrotechnic experiment gone awry. Pyrotechnics had nothing to do with it. Underlord Crowe and the wizard Pettivox, who betrayed us all, built a device – a massive capacitor created, using large amounts of slowsilver, to attract and then imprison the city's magic. The reason, magisters, you have found no evidence of the existence of this device is because it was completely destroyed in the explosion, which also destroyed Dusk House and killed Pettivox.

My apprentice and I have speculated on

the reasons why Crowe attempted this magic thievery. Perhaps it was a move to seize control of the city; perhaps he had plans to weaken our magic for some other purpose. We know that they succeeded in almost depleting the entire city's magic. As you know, Crowe admitted nothing, and has been sent into exile; his reasons, therefore, would seem to be lost to us.

On to magical issues. My fellow magisters, you have made it absolutely clear that you cannot believe my apprentice's theories about the magic of Wellmet. I repeat them to you now: The magic is not a thing to be used, but a living, sentient being which – or perhaps I should say <u>who</u> – serves as a protector of the city of Wellmet. The spells we use to invoke magic are, in fact, the language of this magical being. Our locus magicalicus stones, my fellow magisters, enable us to communicate with the being. Much research remains to be done on the being's actual nature, to discover why it is here in the city, whether other cities are inhabited by similar beings, and to determine what the magic intends for us, the humans who live here.

Whether you believe this theory or not is of no consequence. Do note, however, that as a result of Conn's actions, the city and its magic have been saved from almost certain disaster. The magical levels of Wellmet have stabilized, though I am concerned that the levels remain lower than they were before. Yet despite the fact that Conn sacrificed his locus magicalicus to save the city, you argue that because he no longer has a locus magicalicus he should no longer be considered my apprentice. That is for me to decide, not you.

It is said that only a fool stands in the way of a new idea; I trust, magisters, that there are no fools among you.

Yours sincerely,

NEVERY FLINGLAS

Magister
Heartsease, Wellmet

CHAPTER 2

I blinked the brights out of my eyes. The floor of my workroom was covered with shattered glass and torn book pages. The table lay with its four legs in the air like a dead bug. Smoke and dust swirled around in the corners.

A scrap of charred paper floated to the floor next to me. I squinted at it. A page from Prattshaw's book, the part about contrafusive effects.

The pyrotechnics had worked. The magic had spoken to me again – *without* a locus stone. But what had it said?

Step step tap. I heard the sound of Nevery hurrying up the stairs. He threw open the door. 'Curse it, boy!' he shouted. 'What are you up to?'

I coughed, brushed slivers of glass out of my hair, and got to my feet. 'Just some pyrotechnics,' I said. I looked down at my apprentice's robe. It had a few more scorch marks on it than before.

Nevery scowled. 'A pyrotechnic experiment. I thought you had more sense.' He lowered his bushy eyebrows. 'And where did you come up with the slowsilver, hmmm?'

I shrugged.

More footsteps, and Benet, Nevery's bodyguard-housekeeper, loomed up behind Nevery in the doorway. His knitted red waistcoat and shirt were dusted with flour, and he had a smudge of flour on his fist-flattened nose; he'd been kneading dough. 'He all right?' he asked.

'Yes, I am,' I said. 'Nevery, the magic spoke to me.'

Nevery opened his mouth to shout at me some more, and then closed it. 'Spoke to you? A pyrotechnic effect, then. You were right. Interesting. What did it say?'

'It sounded—' I shook my head. Had the magic sounded *frightened*? But of what? 'D'you know this spell?' I recited the spellwords the magic had said to me: '*Damrodellodesseldeshellarhionvarliardenliesh.*'

'No, boy. I've never heard those spellwords before,' Nevery said. 'Hmmm. Say them again.'

I did, more slowly this time.

He pulled on the end of his beard, frowning, but not at me. 'Something—' he muttered.

'Dinner's ready,' Benet said, and turned to head down the stairs.

'Well, boy,' Nevery said. 'Come along.'

13

We went out and started across the courtyard that lay before Heartsease, Nevery's cane going *tap tap* on the cobblestones.

Heartsease glimmered in the last bits of daylight. It was a wide mansion house built of sand-coloured, soot-stained stone. Most of the house had been missing for a long time, as if someone had taken a huge boulder and smashed a hole through its middle. Blocks of stone and columns and tangled ivy and rosebushes spilled out of the hole, and the roof gaped open to the sky. At one end of the house left standing was my workroom. Nevery's part of the house, along with the kitchen and storage room, Benet's room, and my attic room, was at the other end.

'Nevery,' I asked, 'how did Heartsease get the big hole in the middle of it?'

Nevery gave me one of his keen-gleam looks. 'Quite a point on that question, boy.'

I nodded.

He paused and leaned on his cane. 'Listen, lad. I have experimented with pyrotechnics myself, yes. But be warned. My experiments led to twenty years of exile from Wellmet. This sort of thing' – he pointed with his cane toward my workroom – 'will get you into trouble if you're not careful.' He spun around and swept-stepped away, across the courtyard.

Exile. I didn't want to risk that. But my locus magicalicus had been blown into sparkling dust. That'd left me with no way to talk to the magic, even though I could feel it all the time, looking out for me as it always had.

I didn't have any choice about it; I had to do pyrotechnics, at least until I found a new locus stone.

I started after Nevery and then, from the corner of my eye, caught a glimpse of a black flutter. The big tree in the middle of the court-yard had been empty of black birds ever since last winter, when Nevery and I had destroyed the Underlord's prisoning device and freed the magic. But now something was different. Up in the tree, in the highest branch, perched a single

black shadow, looking down at me with a glinting yellow eye.

'Hello up there,' I called.

The bird shifted on its branch. *Grawk*, it muttered, and looked away.

Just one bird. Had the magic called it back to
keep an eye on things? Had it come because of
the explosion? Would the rest of the birds come
back, too?

Nevery stood in the arched doorway that we
used to get into the house. 'Come along, boy!' he
called.

'Look, Nevery,' I called back, pointing at the
high branch.

Nevery step-tapped back across the courtyard
cobbles. 'What is it?' he said, peering upward.

The night had come on; the black bird was
invisible in the darkness. Never mind.

'Hmph,' Nevery said. 'Come along.'

He crossed the courtyard and led the way inside
and up the narrow staircase to the kitchen, where

Benet had set the table for supper. I sniffed the air, hoping for biscuits and bacon. Fish and – I glanced at the table – stewed greens, pickles, and bread. Mmm. I took off my grey apprentice's robe, hung it on its hook beside the door, and joined Nevery at the table.

Benet thunked a jar onto the tabletop. 'Jam,' he said, then went back to the stove, where he fetched a pan, then scooped a steaming, bony fish onto each of our plates. After clattering the pan back onto the stovetop, he sat down and we started eating.

'You going to do that again?' Benet asked me. He pointed with his chin in the direction of my workroom.

I nodded and picked a bone out of my fish. I could feel Nevery glaring at me. All of a sudden I didn't feel quite so hungry.

Nevery scowled and took a long drink from his mug of ale. 'No, he is not.' He pointed at me with his fork. 'If the magisters find out that you are conducting pyrotechnic experiments, my lad, they will throw you out of the city so fast your head will spin. They have other concerns at the moment, other problems to deal with than one recalcitrant apprentice.'

Right, then I would have to be more careful, that was all.

Staying quiet, I pushed stewed greens around my plate with my fork. I thought about the spell-word the magic had said to me. *Damrodellodessel-deshellarhionvarliardenliesh*. A warning, maybe. But a warning of what? I needed to learn the magic's language. I'd have to look for the spellword in the academicos's collection of grimoires. Or maybe parts of the spellword.

Damrodell . . .

Odesseldesh . . .

Ellarhion . . .

Varliarden . . .

Liesh.

I took a bite of bread and jam and washed it down with a gulp of water. Lady came curling around my feet under the table and I reached down and fed her a few bits of fish.

When we finished dinner, Benet said, 'Water,' so I carried the bucket out to the well in the courtyard and came back, and then helped him clean the plates. Nevery'd gone up to his study. I took an apple and climbed the wide, curving staircase to the next floor. I knew Nevery. Sure as sure, he'd want to shout at me some more about the pyrotechnics.

He was at the table writing a letter. The room was cosy in the pinkish glow of werelights set in sconces on the walls. The ceilings were high and had bits of frothy plaster in the corners; the walls were covered with faded flowery paper. On the floor was a faded, dusty carpet, and the table in the middle of the room was covered with books and papers.

'Nevery?' I said.

'Just a moment,' he said, not looking up.

I took a bite of the apple and went over to

one of the tall windows. It looked out toward the Twilight, the part of the city I'd grown up in. The sky over the Twilight was purple, fading above to black. Only a few lights shone from the dark buildings stacked along the twisted, steep streets. Behind me, Nevery turned the page over and kept writing, the metal nib of his pen going *scritch-scritch* against the paper.

I finished the good part of the apple, then ate the core and flicked the stem out the open window.

Nevery set down his pen and held up the paper to let the ink dry. 'You've been out of school since the Underlord business last winter.'

I had. Because I didn't have a locus stone, the magisters wouldn't let me take apprentice classes at the academicos anymore.

Nevery looked at me from under his bushy eyebrows. 'You need something to do to keep you out of trouble, boy. I'm asking Brumbee to readmit you to the academicos for apprentice classes.' He folded the letter he'd been writing, pulled out his black and shiny locus magicalicus, and muttered a spell, sealing the letter. 'If they'll have you. Brumbee fears you are a bad influence on the other students.' He held the letter out to me. 'I expect you *are* a bad influence on the other students. You've got your keystone?'

The stone to open the magic-locked tunnel gates between the wizards' islands, he meant. I nodded.

'Good. Take this to Brumbee. Don't talk to anyone else. And wait for an answer.'

Brumbee was in the magisters' meeting room, sitting at the long table with his locus magicalicus set in a dish for light, and papers and open books spread all around him. He was writing in another book.

I stood in the doorway, waiting for him to notice me. I'd been in the magisters' meeting room before. Once to spy on them, disguised as a cat; once when they accepted me as Nevery's apprentice and gave me thirty days to find my locus stone; and once after we'd destroyed Dusk House and the terrible device Crowe and Pettivox had built to imprison the city's magic. That time, they'd argued about what had really happened in Crowe's underground workroom and they'd scolded me for losing my locus magicalicus. They didn't seem to understand that destroying the device had made the city's magic work again like they thought it was supposed to, though weaker than before, Nevery said. He measured the magical levels every day with the gauge he had built, and the levels stayed low. We were worried about that, thinking maybe Crowe's device had hurt the magic somehow.

Then I'd told the magisters that the magic was a living being that protected the city. It had been like a pyrotechnic experiment. Take a room full of old croakety-croak magisters, add a new idea, and it was just like combining slowsilver and tourmalifine. They exploded, saying I was an ignorant gutterboy who didn't know any better.

'I do know better,' I'd told them. 'The magic talked to me. It's always protected me, and it protects the city. It's not just a thing to be used, and it needs our help.'

They didn't like that, either. They shouted and shrieked and said I couldn't be an apprentice anymore.

'You're being stupid!' I'd shouted.

Nevery'd sent me out, and I'd stood outside the door shaking and angry, feeling my missing locus magicalicus like a hole in the middle of me, listening to Nevery shouting and Brumbee's worried voice and other sharp voices arguing.

'What is it, Conn?' Brumbee said, looking up from his book and setting down his pen.

I went in and handed him the letter from Nevery.

He spelled it open and read it, shaking his head. 'Oh, dear,' he muttered. He waved his hand at me, still looking at the letter. 'You may sit down while I write a reply.'

My dear Nevery,

When you took Conn in as your apprentice last year, I thought you were doing a good deed, saving a gutterboy from the streets of the Twilight, but now I am not so sure.

His ideas about the magic are simply shocking. The magic a living being? Spellwords a way of communicating with this being? Nevery, you must stop him from thinking about such things. We have enough to worry about at the moment with these strangers lurking around the Dawn Palace and these unexplained attacks on the people of Wellmet. You know as well as I do that something magical must be afoot, for people to be turned into living statues covered with dust! I have spent the last weeks poring over the historical records, seeking a precedent for this kind of magical attack. I have found nothing. It is a very great concern.

But about young Conn. I can see that he feels badly for causing us so much unease with his strange ideas, and with the Underlord troubles last year. He is standing very quiet and subdued beside the meeting room door, waiting as I write this to you; I offered him a chair, but he refused to sit.

I am afraid we cannot readmit him to the academicos at this time. His ideas are too unsettling to the other students. My new apprentice, Keeston, for example, has been talking in most alarming ways about the nature of magic. We cannot allow Conn to take classes with the other apprentices. And even if we do readmit him, he has no locus magicalicus and will never become a wizard.

It's a shame, really. He seems a good boy, despite his odd ideas and the trouble he caused us last year.

Yours,
Brumbee A., Magister,
Master of Wellmet Academicos

CHAPTER 3

I gave Brumbee's letter to Nevery and he spelled it open.

'Hmmm,' he said, reading. 'He won't readmit you to the academicos, Conn.'

Oh. I didn't say anything.

Nevery gave me a keen look from under his eyebrows. 'Well, boy?' he asked.

Not really well, no. I wasn't a

gutterboy anymore, and I needed to be going to school.

'I will give you lessons,' Nevery said.

All right.

I sat up late in the study reading Nevery's grimoire, looking for the spellword the magic had spoken. No luck. Maybe I could get Keeston to nick some books from the academicos library so I could keep looking.

For my first pyrotechnic experiment, I'd nicked tourmalifine and the slowsilver from Nevery's workroom. To do more experiments I'd need more pyrotechnic materials, and that meant finding somebody in the Twilight to sell them to me, and that meant getting my hands on some money. Nevery wouldn't give it to me, sure as sure. I wondered if Rowan would.

The problem with visiting the Dawn Palace, where Rowan lived, was that the guards, especially their captain, Kerrn, didn't like me very much. The first time I'd been there I'd stolen the jewel from the duchess's necklace because it was my locus stone. The duchess didn't like me much, either. If I showed up without an invitation, they'd be likely to slap me in a cell and fill me up with phlister in order to find out what I was up to.

Because I'd been a thief, I was good at getting in and out of places without being seen. I went over the wall at the back of the palace, then, evading more guards than usual, snuck across the formal gardens, through one of the terrace doors, and into the ballroom, which was empty. Rowan's rooms were up two floors and down at the eastern end of the building. I stayed in the servants' hallways, picked a lock to go through an empty room, then eased out into a hallway, down two more doors, and into Rowan's rooms. She had a study, a dressing room, a sitting room, and her bedroom, which had a wide bed in it, and pillowy, comfortable chairs.

She wasn't there. I fetched a book off her bookshelves, flopped onto one of the chairs in the bedroom, and settled down to wait.

I looked up later when Rowan came in. 'Have you been waiting long?' she asked. She was wearing a black wormsilk dress and a student's robe; she'd been at the academicos, where she studied magic, even though she wasn't a wizard. She was the duchess's daughter and needed to know about magical things. Her red hair was tangled, and her fingers were smudged with ink.

I sat up and put the book down. 'Hello, Ro,' I said.

Rowan tossed her bookbag onto her bed and flopped onto the chair next to mine. She glanced sideways at me. 'Are you coming back to school, Connwaer?'

'No,' I said.

'They're still upset with you, then.'

The magisters would never stop being upset with me. I shrugged.

'Mmm. I have a swordcraft lesson in a few minutes.' She bent to untie the laces of her boot.

Get to the point, she was saying. 'Can I have some money?' I asked.

She looked up. 'We-ell, I don't know. What do you need it for?'

I took a deep breath. 'Charcoal and colophony, sulfur and saltpeter. And slowsilver.'

'Explosive materials, I believe.' She sat up straight and gave me her sharp, slanting look. 'From what I hear, my lad, wizards are not supposed to have anything to do with that sort of thing.'

Right, true enough. 'Ro, I don't have any choice.'

'Really,' she said, her voice dry; it made her sound like her mother. 'What are your choices?'

'I have to make some explosions.'

'Indeed,' Rowan said.

'Small ones,' I said.

Rowan pulled off her boot and tossed it toward the door of her dressing room. 'You do have another choice, Connwaer.' She started on the other boot.

'No, I don't,' I said.

'You do,' she said. 'You could choose not to do any pyrotechnic experiments.'

I couldn't abandon the magic like that, not when it needed my help. 'Ro, I'm a wizard. I don't have a locus stone, so I have to find some way to talk to the magic.'

She pulled off her other boot. 'Pyrotechnics?'

I nodded. I knew she'd understand, better than anyone except for Nevery.

There was a knock at the outer door. 'Lady Rowan,' a deep voice called. 'Are you there?'

Rowan sprang up from her chair. 'Just a minute, Argent. I'm just getting ready.' She turned to me. 'My lesson,' she whispered.

Right, time for me to leave. 'Will you give me the money, then?'

She nibbled on her thumbnail, deciding. 'How much do you need?'

'I'm not sure. Maybe eight silver faces,' I said, knowing it was a lot to ask for.

'Is that all?' Rowan said. 'All right. Wait a moment.'

She went into her dressing room. I heard rustlings and the thump of a drawer opening and closing, and then Rowan came out wearing plain brown trousers, a white shirt, a long black coat, and, under the coat, a sword in a scabbard.

Her friend banged at the door again. 'Lady Rowan, are you coming?'

She smiled at me. 'Not today, Argent,' she called. 'I'll meet you at the salle tomorrow afternoon.'

What was she up to?

'I'll give you the money,' she said, showing me a heavy purse string, which she put into her pocket. 'But I'm coming with you.'

Brumbee correct. Boy's ideas about magic shocking. But though boy is stupid about some things, is not stupid about magic. Is likely correct that magic is living being, protector of city, spellwords its language. Magic certainly protected boy when he was living on streets of Twilight. Boy was never sick, had no vermin, did not freeze in the winters; only explanation is that magical being has some kind of bond with him. What that bond is, I do not know.

Twenty years ago, when I conducted my own experiments to see if pyrotechnics enhanced magical spells cast with a locus stone, explosion ripped Heartsease in half. At time, did not understand how I survived. Now think likely that magic protected me as it protected boy when Underlord's device exploded. Wrote *treatise at the time about magical effects, sounds heard when explosion occurred. Wonder if it was magic trying to speak to me.*

CHAPTER 4

Once Rowan and I had snuck out of the Dawn Palace, we headed down the hill toward the Night Bridge. 'Pyrotechnics is illegal,' I said. 'We'll have to go to the Twilight to get what I need.'

Rowan's eyes brightened. 'I've never been there before.'

'Really, never?' I asked.

'My mother says it's too dangerous.'

It wasn't that dangerous. You just had to know where it was safe to go, and where anybody smart would stay away from.

'You've heard about the strange attacks in the Sunrise?' Rowan asked.

Attacks? No. I shook my head.

'The magisters think they have something to do with magic. People have been found covered with dust, turned to stone in their beds, or outside their own front doors. It's dreadful. Surely Nevery's working on a plan to deal with them?' When I didn't answer, she shrugged. 'I suppose you've had your nose in a book and didn't notice.'

I had been busy, true.

We stepped from the cobbled street onto the bridge over the river. Overhead, the sky was grey and the air felt thick with the coming rain. The houses crowded onto the edges of the bridge made the road dark, like a tunnel. A wagon loaded with coal bumped past us, and Rowan shifted to stay out of its way.

'My mother has a point about the danger,' Rowan said. 'Strange shadows have been seen lurking around the palace walls at night. Maybe they have something to do with the killings, but the magisters don't seem to know for sure. The guards chase them, but they always get away.' She glanced at me. 'Captain Kerrn is worried – she's even set two of her guards to look after me when I go across to the academicos. Kerrn's worried that my mother is in danger, too. She thinks the lurkers could be assassins.'

So that's what Nevery had been worrying about; he'd said the magisters didn't want distractions. People turned to stone in their beds sounded something like misery eels, maybe. But I'd never heard of misery eels attacking people out in the street, not even in the worst parts of the Twilight.

And shadowy lurkers. What were they, minions maybe? Had Underlord Crowe come out of exile, back to Wellmet? I shivered; I hoped not.

We came off the bridge and onto Fleetside, the main street leading to Sark Square. A shift was just changing at the factories along the river, so crowds of workers were heading home or in to work at the looms and bottle mills and spinneries.

We wouldn't find anybody at the marketplace who could sell us pyrotechnic materials. I'd have to find somebody to ask, who might know somebody else who might know something about some stranger who might have a bit of blackpowder on hand.

So we turned off the main street onto one of the side lanes in the part of the Twilight called the Deeps. The narrow street was clogged with mud and rubbish, the houses crowding together, and a grimy tavern sign creaking in the autumn wind. Not many people were about – they never were – just a couple of dirty kids, an old woman wrapped in a shawl, and a man carrying a broken-down bedframe on his back. Rowan stared at it all. I had to take her hand and guide her around a muddy pothole, or she would have stepped right into it.

'What's the matter?' I asked.

'I didn't realize it would be this bad,' Rowan said. She was staring at a soot-stained brick house with broken-out windows and a chimney spilling down the side of the roof. A little barefooted girl wearing a raggedy smock stood in the front door, sucking on her finger and watching us with big eyes.

It wasn't so bad. The little girl probably had a mother or father who worked at a factory and brought home money for food. When she got big enough, she would work in a factory, too.

'Come on,' I said. This part of the Twilight was safe enough, but we didn't need to stand around looking like we wanted our pockets picked. I led Rowan down a narrow alley, turned a corner –

– and somebody picked my pocket.

I turned back and – *quick hands* – grabbed the little ragged kid who was trying to slide past me and Rowan. He wriggled and kicked, but he was smaller than I was and not very strong. I held him by the shoulders and shoved him up against the crumbling brick wall to keep him from squirming away. He was a gutterboy, barefoot, dressed in tattery trousers and a man's nightshirt tied with a rope round his waist.

'What's the matter?' Rowan asked. She had her hand on the hilt of her sword, under her coat.

'Get anything?' I asked the gutterboy.

He looked down at his hand. A couple of lock-pick wires. That's what he'd gotten for his trouble. He looked blankly at them and dropped them to the ground. Stupid. A swagshop would've given him a copper lock for them. Oh well; he was probably being stupid because he was hungry.

'If you're going to pick pockets,' I said, 'you have to have quick hands.'

The gutterboy looked up at me; then his glance

skittered over to Rowan, who was watching over my shoulder. He had watery blue eyes and teeth that stuck out. 'Huh?' he said.

'Or you're going to get caught with your hand in somebody's pocket.' And he'd get the fluff beaten out of him if he did. 'Look.' I took a step away from him. 'You come up from behind. Make your feet feathers so the mark doesn't hear you. Then quick-hands in, nick the purse string, and out clean.' I turned to Rowan and lifted the purse string from her pocket to show him how.

'Uh-huh,' he said.

He didn't get it. But he'd get it eventually, or he'd get caught again.

Rowan held out her hand, and I gave her money back. 'I'll let you go,' I said to the gutterboy, 'if you'll help us find somebody.'

'Give me a couple of copper locks, then,' he said.

'Here,' Rowan said. She pulled out her purse string again and gave him a few copper lock coins.

'Now yours,' he said to me.

'I don't have a couple of coppers,' I said.

'Give me one copper, then,' he said.

'I don't have any money,' I said.

'You have to give me something, too.'

I didn't have anything he'd want. Except maybe my coat. Drats. I took it off. 'I'll give you this if you'll help us.'

He looked at it. 'Don't want it.'

'You don't want it *now*,' I said, 'but winter will come in not too long, and you'll really want it then.'

He stared blankly at me.

I sighed. 'If you take it to a used clothes shop, the shop lady will give you money for it, all right?'

He nodded.

'I'm looking for somebody who sells explosives,' I said.

'Give me the coat first,' the boy said.

Right. I handed it over. He put it on; the sleeves hung down over his hands.

'I don't know what explosives is,' he said.

Beside me, Rowan laughed.

'Things that blow up,' I said. His face stayed blank. *'Boom!'* I shouted.

'Oh.' He nodded and picked his nose, then wiped his finger down the front of my coat. His coat. 'Sparks.'

'Yes, sparks,' I said, bending to pick up my lockpick wires; I didn't want to be without them. 'D'you know anybody who makes sparks?'

He nodded again. 'Sparks makes sparks.'

Right. Got it. 'Where does Sparks live?'

'I could show you,' the boy said.

He led us back toward the river, beyond the docks and warehouses and ratty taverns that clustered in the shadow of the bridge. As we walked, the rain started, just a drizzle, and my hair hung down damp in my eyes. A chilly early-autumn breeze blew off the river. Rowan turned up the collar of her long coat. We walked for a long time, out to the mudflats, past the shacks where the mudlarks lived. I'd never been this far out from the centre of the city. The magic was weaker here. Usually I felt it protecting me, like a warm blanket in the wintertime, but here the air felt thin. Most people wouldn't want to live out here, away from the magic. I guessed the pyrotechnist did because otherwise the magic would set off the materials used to make explosions, because the magic liked explosions.

'Here,' the gutterboy said. He pointed at a long, windowless shack with a tar-paper roof and flapping tar paper tacked to its outside walls, and a front yard full of weeds and a scraggly apple tree.

'Thanks,' I said. If I'd had any money, I would've given him some; he looked hungry.

'Yah,' he said, and turned away. Then he turned back. 'Watch out for the Shadows.'

Shadows? Is that what he was calling the dark lurkers? Rowan glanced at me with her eyebrows raised. 'What d'you mean?' I asked.

He shrugged. 'The bad ones,' he said, then spun

and raced away, down the rutted road toward the busier streets of the Twilight.

Shadows. Bad ones. Crowe's former hench-men, sure as sure. His minions. The gutterboy was right, then. I'd better watch out for the bad ones.

CHAPTER 5

'So the lurkers are in the Twilight, too,' Rowan whispered.

'It's probably the old Underlord's minions, Ro,' I whispered back. We stepped up to Sparks's house. The front door was a ragged blanket hung across the doorway.

I pushed the blanket aside and peered in.

Inside was dim-dark. A long workbench was pushed up against one wall. The only light came from a candle stuck in a bowl of water, so the shack wouldn't burn down if it tipped over, I figured. Along the back wall were small barrels piled one on top of the other, and bulging canvas sacks, and scales for weighing things.

Perched on a stool at the workbench was a boy who looked a bit older than Rowan. He was thin and had black hair and was smudged all over with soot, and his skinny-stick legs hung limply down from the stool; they didn't work properly, I guessed. His arms were wiry and strong, though, and, using a pestle, he was pounding something in a wide stone dish. *Pound, pound, pound.* He looked up when Rowan and I came in, scowled, and kept pounding, while staring at us.

From the shadows beside the door came an old woman wearing an ash-grey woollen dress covered with scorch marks. 'What d'you want?' she said in a cracked and ragged voice.

'Are you Sparks?' I asked.

She gave me a gap-toothed grin. 'Yerrrs, I'm Sparks.' She glanced at Rowan, who was looking around the room with wide eyes. 'Howsabout a cup of blackpowder tea?'

All right. I nodded.

'Good for chilly days, blackpowder tea. Be right back, kettle's on the boil. Go an' talk to Embre.' She bustled out of the room.

Leaving Rowan by the doorway, I went over to the boy, who was still pounding. With a name like Embre, he was probably Sparks's grandson. 'Hello,' I said. 'I'm Conn.'

Pound, pound, pound. He paused and looked me up and down. 'I know who you are.'

He did? I shrugged and pointed toward Rowan. 'She's Rowan. What're you doing?' I nodded toward the stone bowl.

Pound.

'What's it—' *Pound.* '—look like?' *Pound.*

I leaned closer to see. It looked like he was crushing black sand into smaller bits of black sand.

He stopped pounding. 'Colophony and charcoal. It's part of an explosive. The smaller the grains' – he pointed at the stuff in the stone bowl – 'the better it mingles with the saltpeter and the sulfur, and the more powerful the explosion is.'

Ah, I'd read about this in Prattshaw. 'What ratio would you use if you wanted a slow explosion?'

He sneered. 'As if I'd tell you.'

Trade secret, I guessed. When I made my own blackpowder, I'd have to check the books and then experiment until I got the right amount of each ingredient.

Sparks bustled back into the room holding a tray with chipped teacups and a teapot on it, which she put down on the table. Her hand, I noticed, was missing two of its fingers. From mixing blackpowder ingredients, I guessed.

'Here you are, love,' she said, pouring out a cup

and passing it to Embre. He took it without looking up and set it on the table.

'And for you, miss.' Sparks handed a steaming cup to Rowan, and then one to me.

I wondered if the tea really had blackpowder in it. I took a sip; it tasted like ordinary tea, but with pepper added. 'Thanks,' I said, and took another sip. Behind me, Rowan sipped her tea, then coughed.

'Whatcha need?' Sparks asked.

'Something to make small explosions I can control,' I said.

'Explosions, is it?' Sparks cocked her head. 'Whatcha need with explosions?'

'I'm a wizard,' I said.

'Are you! From the Twilight and all?' she asked. Embre, I noticed, had put down the pestle and was watching me closely.

I nodded. 'But my locus magicalicus was lost.'

'*Lost?*' Embre interrupted.

'Yes. Destroyed. I need to get the magic to talk

to me, and pyrotechnics is the only way to do that.' Now they would tell me I was crazy. But they needed to know, or they might not let me have the ingredients to make blackpowder.

'Huh,' Sparks said. 'What d'you think?' she asked Embre.

Embre looked me up and down again. 'Twilight needs a wizard,' he said. 'If that's what he really is.'

'Is that so?' Sparks asked, glancing over at him.

He shrugged, then picked up a pencil and started writing on a piece of paper.

'Righty-o, then,' Sparks said. She went to the other end of the dark room and rummaged around for a while, then weighed something on the scale.

Rowan stepped up to whisper in my ear. '*Are* you the Twilight's wizard, Conn?'

'I don't know,' I said. And I didn't. Unless I figured out how to make the explosions work, I wasn't anyone's wizard.

Sparks came back with two canvas sacks. 'Half

noggin of saltpeter, quarter noggin each of sulfur and charcoal and colophony,' she said, setting the bags carefully on the floor. 'And you work out the ratios.'

Embre folded the paper he'd been writing on and tapped its edge against the table. 'No, I've written down the ratios and instructions.' He held out the paper. 'For regular explosions and for slow ones, like you want.'

I blinked. 'Thanks,' I said. I took the paper and put it in my pocket.

Sparks grinned widely, picked up her cup from the table, and slurped at her tea.

'What about slowsilver?' I asked. 'Can you get me some?'

'Ah!' Sparks said. 'Was a big call for slow-silver, much as we could find, round about a year ago.'

Because of Pettivox and the giant magic capacitor device he and Crowe had made in his scheme to steal all the city's magic. I nodded.

'Had to send all the way to Desh for it,' Sparks said.

Desh? I turned to Rowan. I hadn't gotten around to studying geography yet.

'A city far to the east of here,' Rowan said, answering my question. 'It's across a desert, and it was apparently built on sand and a huge slowsilver mine.'

'Yerrrs,' Sparks said, rubbing her three-fingered hand up through her ashy hair. 'But they aren't trading for slowsilver anymore, the Deshans, least-wise not to Wellmet. There's none to be had.'

Embre gave a tiny nod, like he was deciding something. 'They could look themselves. For slowsilver.'

'They could, yes. I can't get down in there,' Sparks said to me. 'And Embre can't, o' course. But you could, and so could your friend here.' She saw that I didn't understand. 'Down in the hole, where the Underlord's Dusk House used to be. Where the explosion was last winter, eh?'

Of course! Why hadn't I thought of that? Pettivox and the Underlord had used a huge amount of slowsilver in their prisoning device. And maybe, after Nevery and I had destroyed the device, some of the slowsilver had been left behind.

Rowan took out her purse string and paid for the blackpowder, and Sparks shoved us outside. The rain was still coming down, and the air smelled like dead fish and mud.

'Go off with you, then,' Sparks said. 'And be careful of the Shadows.'

'We will,' I said.

CHAPTER 6

We'd been warned twice about the bad ones, the Shadows, but I wasn't careful enough.

As we were turning off of Strangle Street, a tall, wide man

with an ugly, lumpy face stepped across the mouth of the alley.

'Look out,' I said. Rowan's hand went to her sword hilt.

I spun around to go back the way we'd come, and another, uglier man blocked us. Minions. Drats. Had Crowe returned? Had he sent them after me? I put my back to the wall as they closed in, and set the canvas sacks of blackpowder materials on the ground.

Rowan drew her sword. 'Stand off,' she said fiercely.

'Business isn't with you, girl,' one of the minions said. He pointed his thumb at me. 'It's with him.'

Rowan stepped in front of me and raised her sword. 'Then your business *is* with me.'

The minion spoke to the other minion over his shoulder. 'Get her out of the way, Hand.'

The other minion, Hand, stepped forward and, before Rowan could slice at him with her sword, grabbed her by the collar of her coat and flung her against the brick wall of the alley across from me; she bounced off the wall and slumped to the ground.

'Ro!' I started toward her, but the minion grabbed me and pinned me to the wall. I kicked him in the shin and tried squirming away, but he thumped me back against the wall until my head spun.

'Keep still. Want a word with you.'

I caught my breath. Just a word?

'You're the lockpick,' the minion said.

I nodded, watching Rowan. She sat on the ground, propped against the wall, her eyes closed. She moved, putting her hand to her head. Her sword lay in the mud next to her feet.

'Little friend of ours told us you were around.'

The gutterboy, he meant. I should've expected it. When I'd lived in the Twilight, most kids without family to look after them earned their bread and bed working for the minions, carrying messages and spying; I'd never done it because the Underlord'd had a word out on me, and because he'd killed my mother. But the gutterboy I'd met earlier didn't have that problem, clear as clear.

'Message for you,' the minion said, stepping closer.

I nodded again. Would it be a message delivered with words or with fists?

'Your name's Connwaer, is it?'

'Yes,' I said.

'A connwaer's a kind of black bird?'

I could guess where he was headed with these questions. I nodded.

'Group of us, Crowe's men, want to talk to you. Warn you off. You figure you're Crowe's right heir, do you?'

I blinked. Crowe was my mother's brother. For a while, when I was a little kid, Crowe had tried locking me in his Dusk House and training me up to be like him. But he'd killed my mother and I'd escaped, and then I'd never had any more to do with him than I had to, and he'd been exiled from the city last winter. 'No,' I said. I looked past him, at Rowan. 'Ro, are you all right?'

She had her head on her knees, but she flapped her hand at me. All right, then.

'Pay attention,' the minion said to me. 'What're you doing in the Twilight?'

I shrugged.

'Right,' he said, his eyes narrowing. 'We reckon you're making a bid to be Underlord. Stirring things up.'

'No, I'm not,' I said.

They waited.

'That all you've got to say?' he asked.

That was all. I nodded.

To my surprise, the minion gave a little bow and stepped aside. Looked like I was going to get off without the minions beating the fluff out of me. My shoulders hunched as I stepped past him, toward Rowan, and sure enough, he grabbed me, his hand heavy at the scruff of my neck.

My heart pounded. 'Is he coming back?' I asked. Crowe, I meant.

The minion let me go. 'Not your business, is it?' He leaned over to whisper into my ear, his breath hot. 'But we'll be watching you, little blackbird.'

Rowan had a bruise on her face and a bump on the back of her head from hitting the wall, but she was all right. She even seemed excited by our run-in with the minions. We headed down the hill toward the Night Bridge, walking fast.

'Those were your Shadows,' I said. I'd slung the sacks of blackpowder ingredients over my shoulder again.

Rowan thought for a moment, then shook her head. 'No, I don't think they were, Conn. The Shadows come out only at night, Captain Kerrn says.' She touched the bruise on her cheek with the tips of her fingers. 'What did those men want with you?'

I shrugged. Old business. She didn't need to worry about it.

After I walked with Rowan back to the Dawn Palace and promised to take her with me the next day, when I went back to Dusk House to look for slowsilver, I went home to Heartsease. I waved to the black bird in the tree, put the bags of blackpowder ingredients in my workroom, then sat at the table in the kitchen, where Benet gave me tea.

'What you been up to?' he asked. He stood at the table, elbow deep in biscuit dough.

'Nothing much,' I said.

Benet snorted.

He kneaded; I drank my tea.

'Currants,' Benet said.

I got up from the table and fetched him a jar of dried currants from the pantry; he added a handful to the dough.

I sat down again and drank more tea. Something about our run-in with the minions wasn't right. The gutterboy had told us to watch out for the

Shadows, and then he'd gone and told the minions where they could find me. Even for someone as stupid as the gutterboy, that didn't make sense. Maybe Rowan was right and the Shadows weren't minions after all.

'Benet,' I said, 'have you heard of anything strange going on in the Twilight?'

'Like what?'

I shook my head. 'I'm not sure. Bad ones or Shadows?'

Benet shaped the dough into biscuits, put them on a pan, and slid the pan into the oven. 'Ask Master Nevery.'

Maybe I would. But first I had to talk to that gutterboy again.

CHAPTER 7

The next afternoon Rowan met me on the Night Bridge. The bruise on her cheek had darkened, but her eyes were sparkling. 'Good afternoon, Connwaer,' she said, with her usual sideways smile.

I grinned at her.

'What adventures await us today, my lad?' she asked.

The smile fell off my face. We had to go to the Dusk House pit. And we had to find the gutterboy.

If he was anything like I'd been when I was a pickpocket, he had his favourite lurking places.

I led Rowan to where the gutterboy had picked my pocket before, the alleyways around Strangle Street. As we went along, I kept my eyes open for minions. The weather was cloudy and a little cold, and I shivered and wished I'd put on the black sweater Benet had knitted for me.

We found the gutterboy after not too long. He was wearing my coat, leaning against an alley wall not too far from Sark Square.

When he saw me and Rowan, he twitched like he might run away, and I got ready to chase him, but he stayed put, his hands in his coat pockets.

'Hello,' I said.

'Hello,' Rowan said.

He stared at us with his scared, watery blue eyes. 'You can't have the coat back,' he said to me.

'I don't want it back,' I said. That wasn't completely true – I wasn't sure Nevery would give me another coat, but I wasn't going to take it back from the gutterboy, either. 'You hungry?' I asked, knowing that he was.

He nodded.

I turned to Rowan. 'Can I have three copper locks?'

She nodded and fished out her purse string, and handed me the coins.

'Watch him,' I said and, keeping an eye out for minions, went over to a stall in Sark Square, used Rowan's money to buy food for us, and came back. I handed him and Rowan a sausage in a biscuit.

He took an enormous bite. Rowan nibbled at hers and then put it in her pocket. I leaned against the wall beside the gutterboy and ate some of my own. 'My name's Conn,' I said.

He glanced aside at me, chewing. 'Yah, I

know. Connwaer, the black bird. I'm Dee.' He took another bite.

'Tell me about the Shadows,' I said.

Dee gulped, and coughed as a bit of food went down the wrong way. 'Shadows?' he gasped.

I nodded. 'You told us to be careful of the Shadows,' I said. 'And you weren't talking about the minions, either.'

'Minions?' he said.

Right. I'd forgotten how stupid this gutterboy was. 'The men who used to be the Underlord's men, the ones you told where to find us yesterday. Not them.'

'I didn't tell them where to find you,' he said quickly.

He was lying. 'I don't care if you did,' I said. 'The Shadows?'

He eyed me for a second, to see if I was going to beat the fluff out of him, which I wasn't. Then he took another bite of sausage and biscuit and chewed it noisily. 'They're bad,' he said.

Yes, I'd gotten that much. 'D'you know what they do?'

'They' – he pointed into the shadowy alley – 'they hide in dark places.'

'They come out only at night?' Rowan asked.

Dee nodded. 'Never in the day.'

'Have they hurt anybody?'

'Yah,' Dee said. 'The men that used to be the Underlord's men? They're worried about 'em. If the Shadows touch you, you turn to stone and then you die. They tried to get an old croak sleeping in an alley outside a smokehole. He fought 'em off with a knife, and they bled black smoke and disappeared.'

That did sound like magic, not minions. 'Anything else?'

He shrugged, ate the last of his sausage and biscuit, and licked his fingers. 'No. That's all. Where they go, they turn things to stone.'

Rowan gave me a sideways glance, her eyebrows raised.

Hmmm. Rowan gave Dee a couple of coppers

for the information and he skiffed off.

'So it is these lurkers, these Shadows, who are responsible for the attacks,' Rowan said. 'Captain Kerrn wasn't sure.'

I wasn't sure Nevery knew about them, either.

We headed towards the top of the hill where the Underlord's mansion, Dusk House, had once stood. I looked over my shoulder. A shadow flitted away into an alley.

Not a Shadow. Dee. The minions had put him onto us, sure as sure.

I hadn't been to Dusk House since Nevery and I had snuck in and I'd helped the magic break out of the terrible device Crowe and Pettivox had built.

'Is this it?' Rowan asked.

I nodded. Before us were the broken and rusting iron gates, and the raggedy edges of the pit where the mansion had been. The ground around it was covered with chunks of brick and stone and twisted bits of metal. Thinking about the house that had once stood there made me shiver. It'd been a hard place to get away from, but the magic had destroyed it and now it was gone forever.

From behind us, I heard sneaking footsteps, *crunch crinch . . . crunch* on the gravelly ground. He wasn't very good at this.

'Hello, Dee,' I said, without turning round.

Rowan turned to look. 'Oh!'

Dee came up, blinking his scared, watery eyes, stealing quick glances at Rowan. 'What're you doing?' he asked.

I wasn't about to tell him; he'd report straight back to the minions. I shrugged.

Rowan looked at me and raised her eyebrows.

Oh, all right. 'We're looking for slowsilver,' I said.

Dee blinked. 'What's slowsilver?'

'It's a contrafusive,' I said, 'when it's combined with tourmalifine.' It was late afternoon and the sun was setting beyond the Twilight. The tumble-down buildings on the steep streets looked like rotted teeth taking a bite out of the light. I took a few steps to the edge of the pit and looked down. Walls hacked out of the stone, a floor far below, scattered with blocks of stone and mortared bricks, and in the corners and cracks, gathering darkness. The shadows looked darker than shadows should, and creepy. Because the prisoning device had been built down there, I reckoned. The magic wouldn't come anywhere near this pit. I didn't want to come anywhere near it either, but I needed the slowsilver.

'Wizards use slowsilver to do magic,' Rowan said to Dee. 'It's hard to find, so we're looking for some here, in the pit.'

Except that we weren't going to look now; it would be dark soon. 'We'd better go,' I said to Rowan.

'Are you coming back tomorrow?' Dee asked.

'Maybe,' I said.

'To look for slowsilver?' he asked.

I shrugged. Sure as sure, he'd run and tell the minions that I was coming back, and I didn't need them lying in wait for me when I did.

Rowan glanced at the setting sun. 'Captain Kerrn will worry if I'm not home soon.'

Leaving Dee, we headed for the Night Bridge and the entrance to tunnels leading to the wizards' islands, walking fast to get there before dark. I kept looking over my shoulder because it felt like we were being followed, but Dee had gotten more careful; I didn't catch a glimpse of him.

Rowan and I went through the tunnels, me opening the gates with my keystone, then I left her at the academicos gate and ran back to Heartsease. I was going to be late for supper!

Home from meeting. Benet said boy and duchess's daughter off somewhere. Growing dark. Worried, curse the boy. These dark lurkers apparently active at night.

Finally, boy came into kitchen, coatless, breathless from running. Should have known boy wouldn't miss supper. Benet had made chicken pie in pot, gravy, carrots, onions. Boy ate seconds, then thirds.

—Well, boy? What have you been up to today?

Boy shrugged.

Benet snorted, handed me teacup. —He was asking yesterday, sir, about Shadows.

Shadows, is it? As good a name as any for these dark lurkers. So the boy has stumbled into it. Magisters trying to keep it quiet, avoid alarming city, but boy very keen. Told him to report. He has found, in Twilight:

Ex-Underlord Crowe's former henchmen nervous

People wary

Shadows seen

'They turn people to stone'

'They bleed black smoke'

Note to self: Must discover whether Twilight has new Underlord, invite to meeting.

CHAPTER 8

After talking to Nevery about what I'd been up to without really telling him anything, I went down to the kitchen.

Benet set aside his knitting and got to his feet. 'Water,' he said. So he could clean the dishes.

I fetched the bucket and went down the narrow stairs to the storeroom door, then outside. Night had fallen. I crossed the cobble-courtyard to the well. Heartsease loomed up behind me, a ragged shadow against the night sky. Beyond the island, the river rushed quietly past, and beyond that, the lights of the Sunrise part of the city twinkled like diamonds against black velvet. The people who lived there were rich and could spend money on lights. The Twilight was dark at night.

Before me, the tree was another dark shadow. I wondered if the black bird was up in its branches, sleeping with its head under its wing.

At the well, I set aside the well cover and dropped its bucket down on its rope. *Splash*, way down in the deeps, and I pulled the bucket up again and poured the water into my own bucket.

As I straightened up, I heard a whisper of wind sliding over the cobblestones. A black rag of shadow hurtled past me; I ducked and turned, water from the bucket slopping down my leg, and saw the bird from the tree, claws out, flapping in the face of a piece of night darker than dark.

It wasn't a man at all, just a man-shaped shadow, swirling and ink black. Where its head would be was a glow of an eye – one blazing eye like a purple-black flame, staring at me.

A Shadow!

It raised a shadow-arm and swept the bird away from its face. Another whisper of wind and a second one was coming round the side of the well, a thing made of smoke and shadow, moving smoothly as if it glided on oiled wheels. Black smoke swirled around it. It swooped at me and its long, shadowy fingers brushed against my arm. I flinched away. Its touch made my arm go numb and heavy, like stone. The smoke flowed over me – no, not smoke but black dust, drier than dead bones.

The Shadow reached again and I whirled around and swung the bucket, which went right through the middle of it, sending rags of shadow swirling. The other one came at me, and I swung the bucket again and let go so that it sent a plume of water flying through the air. The water turned to stone as it struck the Shadow, and fell to the ground with a thud. They came at me again, gliding over the cobbles, their purple-black eyes flaring. I stumbled back toward the house, tripping over a loose stone.

Behind me, the storeroom door opened.

'Benet!' I shouted, scrambling away. 'Shadows!'

I heard a crash, then Benet bulled his way past a Shadow, grabbed me by the scruff of my neck, jerked me to my feet, and pushed me toward the lighted doorway.

'Get Nevery!' he shouted as he turned back, and with a stick of firewood swung at one of the Shadows.

A third Shadow lunged out of the darkness.

'Go!' Benet shouted, and swung the stick again.

I whirled and ran for Heartsease.

Storeroom, narrow stairs, through the kitchen, up the broad stairs to the third floor, and I burst through Nevery's study door.

He was at the table reading, and he looked up as I came in.

'Shadows!' I panted. 'Benet's fighting them!'

Nevery leaped to his feet. 'Where, boy?' he asked, pulling his locus magicalicus from his pocket.

'Courtyard!'

I raced to keep up with Nevery as he strode down the stairs and swept out the storeroom door. Holding up his locus stone, he shouted a few spellwords and then, his voice a booming roar, '*Lothfalas!*'

A wave of light crashed out from his locus stone, washing brightness into every corner of the courtyard. Twinkling blue sparks raced along the branches of the big tree and showered down onto the cobbles.

Across the courtyard, three dark figures were

crouching over Benet, who lay still on the ground; as the light washed over them, they flinched back, then reeled away, disappearing with a flutter of black dust down the steps to the tunnel.

Nevery shouted another spellword and a wind leaped out of the air and chased the Shadows, whooshing down the tunnel after them.

Blinking the brights from my eyes, I started across the cobbles to Benet.

He was stone-still.

'Quick, lad,' Nevery said as he came up, shoving his locus stone into his pocket, plunging us into darkness. 'Get his feet.'

Nevery heaved up Benet's shoulders and I picked up each of his heavy legs, and we trundled him into the storeroom and up to the kitchen.

'Fetch blankets,' Nevery ordered, 'and my grimoire.' I set down Benet's legs and ran for my room, grabbed the two blankets off my bed, then stopped to pull two more blankets from a wooden chest on the stairway landing. I brought them down to Nevery, then raced back up to his study for the grimoire. His spell book was fat, held closed with a lock because it was bursting with paper markers and dried leaves and interesting bits of maps.

Nevery snatched the grimoire from my hands and spelled it open. 'Let me see,' he muttered. Then he found the page he was looking for. Glancing at a spell in the book, he laid his locus stone against Benet's forehead and muttered spellwords.

I caught a look at Benet's face. It was grey, and his lips were darker grey, and he was still as stone. He *was* stone. Nevery kept saying the spell, and I laid blankets over Benet.

Then I crouched beside Nevery. 'Will he be all right?' I asked. I wasn't sure Benet was even breathing. I picked up his hand. It was stiff and heavy.

'I don't know, lad,' Nevery said softly. 'I used a spell that animates stone. It is meant to make statues dance, for entertainment. I do not know if it will work for this purpose.' He rested his hand on Benet's forehead.

Benet lay still for hours. I brought up wood from the storeroom and we built up the fire. Nevery sat in a chair and I stayed next to Benet, holding his stone hand.

'They were not human,' Nevery said, looking up from his book.

The Shadows, he meant. No, they hadn't been.

'Creatures of magic,' Nevery said.

I nodded.

Then we were quiet, waiting.

Finally, with the sound of one stone grinding across another, Benet took a deep, shuddery breath. His eyes cracked open, then closed again. He started to shake and shiver as the stone magic wore off, his teeth clickety chattering.

'Tea,' Nevery said.

The kettle had a little water in it, so I added a few sticks to the stove to make the kettle boil, then got out the teapot and leaves. When the tea was ready, I poured out a cup and brought it back to Nevery.

'Hold it for him,' Nevery said, and raised Benet's head.

I brought the cup to Benet's grey lips so he could get a sip, then gave him another, and another. He kept shaking and didn't open his eyes.

'I need to check something,' Nevery said. 'Watch him carefully, boy.'

I nodded; I would.

Nevery swept-stepped out of the room, his locus magicalicus flaring into light as he spoke the lothfalas spell.

Benet lay shivering, and I held his hand, which was still heavy as stone.

After a long time, the storeroom door slammed and Nevery came upstairs. First he came to the hearth to check Benet, and then he sat down at the table. 'Tea, boy,' he said.

I laid Benet's hand down and went to the stove, poured tea into a cup, put it on a saucer, and brought it to Nevery.

'Are they gone?' I asked.

'Yes,' Nevery answered. He took a long drink of tea. 'Put some honey in this.' He held out the cup.

I added honey and brought it back to him.

Nevery tasted it and nodded. 'I'd like to know why the Shadows came here and how they got through the Heartsease gate.'

I shook my head. Then I stopped and thought about it. The creepy feeling I'd had at the Dusk House pit. Maybe it wasn't because of the device and Pettivox and the Underlord. Maybe it was because the Shadows had been hiding there, watching us.

That meant they could've found Heartsease by following me and Rowan back from the Twilight. And it meant the Shadows Nevery had chased off could be heading back to the pit. And if they were hiding in the pit, then they might've found –

– Dee.

CHAPTER 9

'I have to be sure he's all right,' I said. Sure as sure, Dee was stupid enough to stay at the Dusk House pit after dark.

'Who is all right?' Nevery asked.

'Dee. The gutterboy. We left him at the pit where Dusk House used to be. I think the Shadows are hiding there.'

Nevery lowered

his bushy eyebrows. 'What were you doing at Dusk House?'

Oh, he was not going to like this. 'Well, Nevery, I was looking for slowsilver.'

'Curse it, boy!' Nevery shouted. He glanced over at Benet and lowered his voice. 'You are not to do any more pyrotechnic experiments.'

'But what about Dee?' I asked.

Nevery nodded. 'I see why you'd want to protect this gutterboy, but if the Shadows are laired in the remains of Dusk House it's far too dangerous.'

'I can take care of myself, Nevery,' I said.

'I'm sure you can, but these Shadows are creatures of magic and you are not equipped to deal with them. I must alert the magisters; we will deal with it. And I cannot go with you; Benet cannot be left as he is.'

'What if I go in disguise?' I asked. 'You could do the embero spell. I'll be safe enough as a cat. I could make sure Dee's all right and then come home.'

Nevery set down his teacup. 'No.'

'Then I'll go as I am,' I said, and started for the door.

Nevery stood up and slammed his fist on the table; his teacup jumped in its saucer. 'I said no, boy! I will lock you in your room if I have to.'

I turned to face him. 'If you do that, Nevery, I'll pick the lock to get out.' I started for the door again.

'Stop!' Nevery roared. He glared.

I glared back at him.

Then he sat down, as if he was suddenly tired. 'Curse it,' he muttered, shaking his head. 'Very well. I will cast the embero.'

Nevery fetched his grimoire and opened it to the page with the embero spell written on it in tiny, neat letters. For a while Nevery studied the spell so he could say it smoothly, and I stood before him, jittering a bit with impatience.

The embero spell was very good for sneaking. Nevery had used it on me before, to turn me into

87

a cat for spying on the magisters, and I'd used it myself to sneak into the Underlord's mansion. The best thing about the embero, though, was that when I turned into my characteristic creature, a cat, I had a quirked tail.

'Very well,' Nevery said at last, and closed the grimoire. 'Keep still, boy.' He placed his locus magicalicus against my forehead and started the embero.

The magic burned out from his locus stone, flashing through me and throwing sparks before my eyes. The room tilted, and I crashed to the floor and everything went dark.

And then, just as suddenly, it went light again. I hopped to my feet. While I'd been out, Benet had woken up. He sat propped in a chair, hunched over and shivering, and staring at me.

Nevery was staring, too, and pulling on the end of his beard. 'Very odd,' he said.

'D-d-d-did you change the sp-p-pell, sir?' Benet asked, his teeth chattering.

'No,' Nevery said. 'It should have been exactly the same as before.'

I tried to give my tail a twitch – it felt funny – and then pounced at Nevery's foot.

And I went sprawling, no quirked tail keeping me balanced. No four paws, either.

Oh, no.

'You'd better have a look, boy,' Nevery said, and got up from his chair to fetch a mirror. He brought it down to the floor for me to look into.

Drats.

A black bird, not a cat. The embero spell wasn't supposed to work like this. I cocked my head to see better, first one eye, then the other. The embero had turned me into a connwaer, a scruffy one, with black feathers, a ruffled black crest, and bright blue eyes. I lifted a wing and the feathers fanned out.

Hmmm. Wings might be as good as any cat's tail.

Nevery lifted the mirror away. I eyed Benet's shoulder, high above me. I might be able to fly to it. *Hop, hop, jump*, and I flapped my arm-wings up and down and went tumbling, beak over tail feathers, across the floor.

Nevery gave a snort of laughter. I hopped to my feet and shook my feathers back into place. Try again.

Up I jumped, and this time I scooped at the air with my wings and made it to Benet's blanket-covered knee, then scooped again and flapped to his shoulder. My balance was off, and I clung tightly, flapping a little and flipping my tail feathers.

'Mind the c-c-claws,' Benet said. Through my bird feet I could feel him shaking.

I relaxed my grip and settled, folding my wings.

'Well, boy,' Nevery said. 'You're going?'

I dipped my head. *Yes*.

'Go and look for this friend of yours, then, and come straight home.' Nevery bent and held out his arm and I hopped onto it, clinging to the black cloth of his coat sleeve. 'I'll take you outside.'

He carried me down the stairs, through the

storeroom door, and, after kindling his locus stone, went out into the night. When he reached the middle of the courtyard, he asked, 'Ready?' and before I could open my wings he swung his arm, tossing me into the air.

My bird bones were so light that I tumbled away from him, then caught the air with my wings and wobble-flapped into the air, higher and higher, until I reached the courtyard tree. Leaves and twigs lashed at me; I ducked and flap-flopped and landed on a wide branch using my tail to catch my balance.

'You all right, boy?' Nevery shouted up.

Yes, I called back. It came out as 'Awk!'

Down below, Nevery looked small; he shook his head, turned, and swept-stepped across the courtyard, back into Heartsease, taking the locus light with him. I clung to the branch with my clawed feet and looked around. My connwaer eyes could see far into the sharp-edged shadows. Two branches away perched the other black bird, the one the magic had been using to watch me, I guessed. I saw its yellow eye, glinting in the darkness.

Grawk, it muttered.

I wasn't going to sit around chatting with it.

I hopped up from branch to branch until I got to the top of the tree, a launching place. Trying not to think about what I was doing, I threw myself from the branch and tumbled down, then caught the air with my wings and flap-flapped until I'd straightened myself out. I aimed my beak toward the dark, steep streets of the Twilight.

My wings were growing tired by the time I got to the Dusk House pit, a deep, shadowy, darker place in the ground.

I glided in a rough circle to the edge of the pit, where I skidded to the ground in a swirl of feathers – I wasn't good at landing yet – and then hopped up to perch on a chunk of stone. Cocking my head, I listened.

The night was completely still. Behind me,

streaks of grey lightened the dark sky; dawn was coming. I shifted, and a pebble rolled away and bounced down into the pit, echoing.

I leaned forward, opened my wings, and jumped, and felt the rush of wind lifting me. Slowly, I spiralled toward the bottom of the pit, down into the darkness. I splat-landed on a brick.

Silence. No sign of the Shadows. The stone walls of the pit loomed all around. Way overhead the sky lightened to grey. I hopped to the ground, onto the cracked stone that had been the floor of the Underlord's workshop, where he and the wizard Pettivox had built the prisoning device. I took a few hopping steps, then stopped to listen again. Nothing.

The dawn light hadn't reached this far into the pit; the cracks and corners were still deep in shadow, but my connwaer eyes could see into them, and saw that they were empty.

But the Shadows had been there.

At first I thought it was a bundle of rags. Then

I recognized my coat.

My bird heart fluttered. I hop-flapped closer.

Dee.

He lay curled up like he was asleep, with my coat over his shoulders as a blanket, but he was too still. His skin was grey. Overhead the sky turned pink. A beam of light from the rising sun crept down one wall of the pit. I hopped onto his bare foot. He didn't move. I hopped up to his face and with my beak, pecked at his hardened skin. His lips were grey and cold.

The morning light crept across the floor, and high above, the warm sun peeked over the edge of the pit.

But Dee stayed cold. He was dead.

CHAPTER 10

By the time I got home to Heartsease, my wings ached with tiredness. In the brightening day, Nevery stood in the courtyard, watching the sky. As I spiraled raggedly in, he raised his arm, a landing place. I back-flapped, perched, and lost my balance, tumbling to land *splat* on the cobblestones.

'All right, lad.' Nevery crouched down beside me and smoothed my feathers, then brought his huge hand, holding his locus magicalicus, up to my bird-face. His voice murmured the reverse embero. The spell crashed into me, and I went out.

When I opened my eyes, Nevery was standing beside me and the sun was shining. 'Come inside,' he said.

I followed him in, trudging up the stairs to the kitchen. Benet sat wrapped in his blankets, still shaking.

'You all right?' I asked.

'Fine,' he said, and picked up his knitting with stiff hands.

Nevery handed me a cup of tea; I went over to sit on the floor beside the fireplace.

'Well, boy?' Nevery said, taking a seat at the table.

I put my teacup down on the floor. 'Dee's dead.'

'The Shadows?'

My voice caught in my throat. I nodded.

We sat without speaking. Benet's knitting needles went *c-c-clickety-tick*. My tea got cold.

Nevery sighed and got to his feet. 'You rest, boy, and I will use my scrying globe to call a meeting. Then we will go to Magisters Hall.'

I went up the stairs to the fourth floor, then climbed the ladder to my attic room. The sun beamed in through the three small windows that looked out over the courtyard, and west toward the Twilight. My bed was just a bare mattress; I'd left my blankets down in the kitchen. I lay down and tried to sleep. Every time I closed my eyes I saw the swirl of black dust or the purple-black glow of the Shadow's single eye.

The day before, on our way back from the Twilight, Rowan and I had talked about Dee.

She'd started out talking about Embre. 'Poor Embre,' she'd called him.

'What d'you mean?' I'd said.

Rowan shook her head. 'He lives in that broken-down shack, and he can't use his legs.'

'He does all right,' I said. No, Embre did better than all right. He was smart, he had Sparks, and he knew his business.

'And poor Dee, too,' Rowan had said. 'Before this, I didn't quite understand what it meant to be a gutterboy.'

Dee did have a hard time of it, I'd thought. But he was working for the minions, and that meant they'd be looking after him, and one day, if he grew big enough, and mean enough, he'd become a minion himself.

Except that now he wouldn't.

'He was wearing that coat,' Rowan had said. 'The one you gave him. It made me realize – you were like Dee, weren't you?'

'I was nothing like Dee,' I'd told her.

I lay in my bed with tiredness covering me like a prickly blanket and looked up at the sloped ceiling, the cracked white-grey plaster, the spiderwebs in the corners. The air smelled of the ashes left in the hearth; from outside I heard the faint sounds of Benet in the courtyard chopping wood, and the *rushrushrush* of the river.

When I'd lived in the Twilight I *had* been just like Dee. I'd never thought about anything except where to find something to eat or a warm corner to sleep in, or how to keep the minions from beating the fluff out of me. If the magic hadn't been protecting me, I would've ended up like Dee, too – frozen on a doorstep, maybe, too stupid to have picked a wizard's pocket and become a wizard myself.

Now Dee was dead and – I had to face up to it – it was partly his own stupid fault, but it was my fault, too.

Tap tap tap.

I opened my eyes. The sun still shone brightly into my room; I hadn't slept for very long.

Tap! Tap! I sat up in bed, blinking. *TAP! TAP!* Nevery, banging with the knob of his cane on the trapdoor that opened into my attic.

'Are you awake, boy?' he called.

I went over to the trapdoor and opened it. At the bottom of the ladder Nevery peered up, looking cross.

'I'm up,' I said.

'Well, come along,' Nevery said. 'The meeting begins soon.'

'Coming,' I said, and went to the trunk at the end of my bed to get my black sweater, the one Benet had knitted for me, and pulled it on over my head. When I climbed down the ladder Nevery had already gone, so I ran down the stairs after him. As I passed through the kitchen, Benet handed me a biscuit.

'Thanks!' I said, and raced after Nevery. He was already halfway across the sunlit cobbled courtyard, heading for the tunnel.

He gave me his keen-gleam glance as he strode along. 'Well, boy?'

Not really well, no. I shoved the biscuit into my pocket. We got to the stairs and went down.

'Now, this meeting,' Nevery said.

I nodded.

'Keep quiet unless you're spoken to. Don't ask any questions. Do *not* bring up your ideas about the magic. Don't cause any trouble.' Nevery muttered something else into his beard, but I didn't hear what he said.

Nevery was right to be worried about the meeting. Captain Kerrn was there, looking fierce, and the duchess, and the magisters, who, when they saw me follow Nevery into the meeting room, argued that I shouldn't be allowed in.

Nevery ignored them and started the meeting. When he told me to, I stood at the end of the table and told them about Dee, that the Shadows had turned him to stone.

They didn't believe me. Trammel said, 'This Dee person was a gutterboy. How can we be sure he didn't just die of a fever?'

I told them I knew what stone looked like, and argued with them until they were shouting at me, and then Nevery stepped in. He told them about how the Shadows had attacked me, and then Benet, in the courtyard outside Heartsease, and how the lothfalas spell had defeated them.

'Then you have actually seen these – these *Shadows*?' Brumbee asked in a shaking voice. 'And they are not ordinary men?'

'I have seen them, yes,' Nevery said. 'I posit that the Shadows used magic to get through the Heartsease gate. I am certain that they themselves are creatures of magic, and not men at all.'

'Well then,' said Brumbee, 'what could they possibly be?'

'I do not know,' Nevery said, shaking his head. 'They seem to be made of smoke and shadow. I have never heard of anything like this.'

'Might we have an enemy from outside the city?' Trammel asked.

'We must!' Brumbee said. 'No one from within the city could send such terrible creatures against us.'

'Wellmet is under attack!' the bat-faced magister, Nimble, said. 'What will we do?'

'Oh, dear,' Brumbee said. 'We shall have to study the situation further, of course, before we do anything.'

The duchess stood up from her seat at the other end of the table. She wore a dark green dress with a high collar, and had her red-grey hair braided in a crown on her head. As she looked sternly around at the magisters, they quieted. 'If Wellmet is under attack, we must defend ourselves. Magister Nevery, your use of this light spell to deter them seems to corroborate what the unfortunate gutterboy told Connwaer, and what Captain Kerrn has suspected: the Shadows fear light and thus come out only after dark. We must, therefore, institute a curfew.'

Kerrn nodded. 'My guards could enforce a curfew. We would have everyone off the streets of the Sunrise before dark.'

I took a deep breath. Nevery had warned me

not to make trouble. 'What about the Twilight?' I asked.

They all stared. They'd forgotten about me, standing at the end of the table.

'Shouldn't you make a curfew in the Twilight, too?' I said. 'Dee might not've been killed if he'd been told to get off the streets. And people in the Twilight work shifts at the factories at night. They're in danger, too.'

The duchess nodded, though when she looked at me she frowned. 'This is true.'

Kerrn said, 'We would need to coordinate a curfew with the Underlord, but no Underlord has arisen to take Crowe's place.'

'Do what you can with the guards you have,' the duchess said. 'Now we must turn our attention to other solutions. I wish to discuss with you diplomatic missions to our neighbouring cities, to see if they are having similar problems.'

From his seat halfway down the table, Nevery

caught my eye and nodded toward the door. Time for me to go out.

Kerrn followed me out into the hallway; two of her guards were there, too, waiting for the duchess. As soon as the meeting hall door closed behind her, Kerrn grabbed me by the front of my sweater, dragged me down the hall, and shoved me up against a wall. Her guards came and stood behind her, arms folded, scowling.

'The Lady Rowan's safety is my responsibility,' she growled into my face. Her long blonde braid hung over her shoulder like a rope and her ice-chip blue eyes glinted. 'You took her unguarded into the Twilight, thief.' With her strange accent, she made *Lady Rowan's safety* sound like *Lady Rrrrowan'sh shafety*.

'She was safe enough,' I said. And I hadn't taken her; she'd taken herself.

'Safe?' Her grip tightened. 'You say *safe*? She left her guards behind. She was with that gutterboy just before he was killed by Shadows. She came home with a bruise on her face. She was not *safe enough*. The duchess agrees. She gives me a message to give to you. Stay away from the Lady Rowan – do not speak to her or write to her.' She leaned closer and lowered her voice. 'And I have another message, thief. From me. Stay away from the Dawn Palace. If my guards catch you, they will lock you in one of my cells and not even your master Nevery will be able to get you out.'

Down the hall, the meeting room door opened and people came out, talking. Then *step step tap*, *step step tap*. Nevery, coming along the hallway, his knob-headed cane tapping on the stone floor.

'Do you understand?' Kerrn whispered.

I nodded.

'Good.' She thumped me once against the wall, then let me go, straightened, and, followed by her guards, strode away toward the meeting hall door to meet the duchess.

Nevery came up, leaned on his cane, and gave me one of his keen looks. 'Well, boy?'

I shrugged.

'Talking with Captain Kerrn about the weather, were you?'

'Nevery, if I ever go missing come look for me in Kerrn's jail cells,' I said. Just in case.

'Hmph. Come along.'

Nevery and I passed down into the damp tunnel under the river, the light from his locus magicalicus flickering on the dripping walls. He spoke an opening spell and we went through a gate, heading for Heartsease. 'That was well done, Conn,' he said, 'to remind us of our responsibility to the Twilight.'

Maybe. But reminding wasn't enough. 'Nevery,' I said. 'There's something I have to do.'

'Very well,' Nevery said. 'Be back before dark, boy.'

I would try.

On the Twilight side of the bridge I headed straight for the marketplace. In the Sunrise part of the city, where the streets were wide and well-lit and everybody got enough to eat, the guards were making sure the people were safe in their houses. Here in the Twilight, shadows were gathering in corners, and the blank, broken windows of the houses watched me as I walked up the steep streets.

Sark Square was almost deserted, only a couple of stalls open. I remembered the biscuit in my pocket, the one Benet had given me before the meeting, and I pulled it out and took a bite, leaning against a wall, the bricks still warm from the day's sunlight. The biscuit had butter and jam on it.

Across the square, I saw a ragged kid say something to a man, who looked where the kid pointed and saw me. He nodded and headed off down a side street. I ate the last of my biscuit and watched the sun dip behind the houses; the sky turned orange, then darker red.

I was just straightening up from the wall, ready to head home, when the two minions who had jumped me before came into the square, saw me, and came over. Part of me wanted to run away, but I stilled my twitching feet and stayed put.

'You want to talk to us, blackbird?' the uglier one said.

I nodded. 'What're you called?' I asked.

The minion narrowed his eyes. He waited for a moment, then nodded at his friend, who was holding a burlap sack. 'He's Hand.' He showed me his fist. 'I'm Fist.'

Fist, right. Good name. 'You know about Dee?' I said.

Fist nodded. 'We know.'

'He was killed by the Shadows,' I said.

'Figured,' Fist said; behind him, Hand nodded.

'You know the Shadows only come out at night. Over in the Sunrise they're making a curfew. No one's allowed out after dark, for safety.'

'An' you come to tell us that you think the Twilight needs a curfew?' Fist asked.

I nodded.

'You see anybody around, little bird?' the minion said.

Now that he mentioned it, the streets were empty; everyone from the marketplace had gone

109

home. The minions had set their own curfew. And the sun was just about down; I needed to get back to Heartsease.

'Right, good,' I said quickly. I edged away from Fist.

'Hold up,' he said, moving to block me.

Drats. Now they were going to beat the fluff out of me for coming back to the Twilight after I'd been warned off.

Fist nodded at Hand. 'Give it to him.'

Whatever it was, I didn't want it.

'No harm,' Fist said. 'We found this on him.' Hand pulled something out of his sack.

On Dee, he meant. My coat. Brown, with black buttons, patches on the elbows, and frayed edges along the hem. Hand held it out to me, and I took it.

I put it on. Dee had rolled up the sleeves; I rolled them back down again so it fit me, and put my hands into the pockets.

The pockets were full of dust.

Interesting clue to Shadows. Boy found black dust in pockets of coat worn by gutterboy when killed. Have analysed dust. Very fine, light, almost oily in texture. Not found anywhere in Wellmet. From outside.

Need to find expert on geography to consult, discover where dust comes from. Have called meeting with magisters, will bring dust, see what they think.

CHAPTER 11

While Nevery was at another meeting, I went up to the study to look at some more grimoires to see if I could find the spellword the magic had spoken to me. It might be something about the

Shadows, so I needed to figure out what it meant sooner than soon.

I pulled one dusty, thick book off the shelf, and heard a papery *crackle*. Standing on tiptoes, I peered into the space where the book had been. Something was in there, shoved into the space behind the other books. I reached in and pulled it out. Two bundles of dusty papers, one tied with string, the other tied with a faded red ribbon. The one tied with string was a sketch of a map with things called *dragonlairs* labelled on it in old, swirly script. I set it aside to look at it later. Then I untied the ribbon-tied bundle and unrolled the papers. A treatise. Nevery had written it; I recognized the tiny, neat handwriting.

An Examination of the Enhancement of Magical Effects
Through the Application of Pyrotechnics

Well, that could be interesting.

I didn't want Nevery coming back to find me

reading it, so I went to my workroom. My bags of blackpowder ingredients were next to the door. The floor was still sprinkled with crumbs of glass and shredded papers from my pyrotechnic experiment. The air smelled smoky. I crunched over to the window and opened it, and lifted the table onto its four legs. Then I pulled the chair over, sat down, and started reading.

After a while, the black bird from the courtyard tree flew over and perched on the window frame.

Nevery's treatise was about using pyrotechnics along with a locus magicalicus to do magic. He'd done experiments with the lothfalas spell and had found that if he set off a tiny explosion while saying the spell *and* holding his locus magicalicus, the resulting light was brighter. He spent pages and pages calculating how much brighter; I didn't see much point in that. At the end he'd made notes about what he called *odd pyrotechnic effects*, like the fact that he'd heard *unexplained sounds* during the explosions. The magic talking back to him, clear as clear, but he hadn't realized it.

I set the papers aside and eyed the bags of blackpowder ingredients by the door. With the Shadows' attack on Dee and the meeting with the magisters, I hadn't had time yet to test Embre's recipe.

I fetched my apprentice robe from its hook beside the door and put it on. Then I set the noggin of saltpeter at one end of my worktable, the noggin of sulfur at the other end, and the noggin of charcoal across the room on a bookshelf. I didn't want the magic knocking them over and making them mingle.

The bird hopped off the window frame onto the tabletop, then hopped up to perch on top of the noggin of sulfur.

'Be careful,' I told it.

It cocked its head and looked at me with its yellow eye. *Grawwwwwk*, it muttered.

I got out the paper Embre had written for me. His handwriting was neat and straight.

Blckpwder Expl.

Use highest quality materials.

Warning: MUST keep materials apart or will spontaneously combine & combust.

Keep charcoal dry.

Sulfur emulsion:

In saucer cmbn two spnsful dry fine charcoal, one spn sulfur.

Hold saucer over low candle flame to count of twenty, mix with glass rod, add pinch colophony, hold to flame count thirty, mix with rod. Cool. Result: emulsion clear black. If clouded, do over, be sure saucer clean, charcoal dry.

For slow explosion:

Stir emulsion. Add one cupful saltpeter.

Ratio 15:3:2, alter slightly for diff. rate.

Good luck.

I got to work. The charcoal was dry, and every time I measured some out, it stuck to my fingers and to the spoon I was using to measure it. The sulfur smelled awful, and the saltpeter smelled even worse, like a back-alley cesspool in the Twilight. When I put the sulfur and the charcoal together, they didn't want to mingle properly.

I cleaned off the spoon and started again.

After a while, footsteps came up the stairs to my workroom. Not Benet or Nevery. With a flutter, the black bird left its perch and flapped away, back to the tree, I guessed.

'Hello, Conn,' Rowan said from the doorway.

I didn't look up. I wasn't supposed to talk to her.

'I'm not supposed to talk to you,' Rowan said. 'But I wanted to see what you were up to.' She paused. 'Conn, I'm very sorry about Dee.'

I nodded, and swallowed down a lump of sadness.

Rowan came farther into the room. 'What are you working on?'

I pointed at the saucer. The emulsion I'd made was cloudy; I was going to have to start again.

'What is it?'

I handed her Embre's recipe. While she read it, I set aside the cloudy emulsion and used a rag to clean off a new saucer.

'I see,' Rowan said, setting the paper on the table. 'Pyrotechnics again? What, exactly, do you hope to accomplish, aside from blowing your fingers off?'

I shrugged. I wasn't sure. Even before my pyrotechnic experiment, probably since the Shadows had come to Wellmet, the magic had felt different — it felt frightened, and it made me feel jittery, too. I had to find out what it was afraid of. The Shadows, sure as sure, but if they were creatures of magic, somebody else had made them, and the Wellmet magic was afraid of that, too.

I knew how to find out what it was. If the magic could talk to me during a pyrotechnic explosion, then maybe I could talk to it. I could say magical words, and it would know I was trying to help it, even if it couldn't understand me.

Rowan was quiet for a few moments. 'You're not going to talk to me, are you?'

I shook my head.

'Mmm. My mother was very angry. I tried to explain that going to the Twilight was my idea, but she blames you for taking me there. She's starting to think that the magisters are right about you, and Captain Kerrn is trying to convince her that you should be arrested.' She pointed at the saucer of sulfur emulsion. 'You need to be careful, Conn. You should stop doing these experiments.'

I shook my head again.

'Don't be stupid!' she said.

I opened a book and stared down at the page, not seeing the words. Rowan didn't know what it was like to lose a locus magicalicus. Or to have the magic talk to her and not be able to answer back. I closed the book and set it aside. My hands were shaking; I bumped the saucer of sulfur emulsion, and it slopped onto the tabletop. Drats. I blotted it up with the sleeve of my robe.

Rowan stood there for a moment, watching. Then she said, 'Well, I can see you're busy, and guards are waiting for me in the courtyard.'

I didn't answer.

'I'd better go, then.' She paused. 'Connwaer, your arm is smoking.'

I looked down. The sulfur emulsion had eaten a hole in my sleeve, and a thin line of grey-black smoke trickled up. Drats! I pulled off my robe and threw it to the floor, then stamped out the smoke. When I looked up, Rowan was gone.

CHAPTER 12

That night after supper, Nevery and I were at work in his study — he was reading a book, and I was trying to keep my eyes open long enough to check one of the old grimoires for the spellword the magic had spoken to me during the

explosion. Lady the cat sat on the table, curled up on an open book.

Downstairs, the storeroom door slammed and heavy footsteps came running up the stairs.

Benet burst into the room. 'Message from Captain Kerrn,' he said. 'The Dawn Palace is under attack!'

I stood up, blinking the sleep out of my eyes.

'Shadows. No one else could get through those defenses,' Nevery growled, getting to his feet. 'My robe and cane, Benet, at once.' He frowned across the table at me. 'I don't suppose there's any point in ordering you to stay home.'

I didn't see much point in it, no.

We got ready and headed out the storeroom door, Nevery striding across the cobbled courtyard with his cane and locus stone, Benet with his truncheon. Me with . . .

'Nevery,' I panted, running to catch up with him.

'What,' he said, not sparing me a glance.

'I have to get something from my workroom.'

Nevery stopped. 'Make it fast, boy.'

Right. I raced across the courtyard to the other end of Heartsease and up the stairs to my workroom. It was dark; I knocked over a chair, then bumped into the table. I felt over the tabletop until I found what I was looking for – a stoppered vial of sulfur emulsion – and put it in my coat pocket. Then to the bookshelf, where I'd put one of the noggins. I reached in and grabbed a handful of saltpeter and shoved it into my other pocket.

Now I'd be ready to fight Shadows.

We came through the gates of the Dawn Palace. On the wide front steps, a line of guards and a magister – Trammel – fought a darting, swooping crowd of Shadows. Trammel's locus magicalicus cast a circle of weak light around the guards, who carried swords and pikes.

As we came nearer, the Shadows surged forward like boiling black smoke, and the guards on the steps fell back toward the front doors. A guard had fallen, and one of the other guards dragged her by the collar away from the Shadows.

'Stay with me, boy,' Nevery said. Followed by Benet, he strode toward the fight.

I hung back.

This wasn't right. I knew how to get into the Dawn Palace, and it wasn't by attacking the front doors.

It was over the wall and through the glass doors at the back of the palace. A guard ran past me, shouting; I looked in the direction he was going and saw Nevery, striding into a swarm of Shadows, swinging his knob-headed cane, and Benet with his truncheon.

Lothfalas! I heard Nevery shout, and his locus stone flared into light. The Shadows fell back, and then they attacked again.

He was busy.

I headed away from the fight. The sound of the guards' shouts faded as I came round the corner of the palace and into the formal gardens at the back. The windows were all dark; the garden was dark; I saw humps that were bushes, and the faint glimmer of white gravel on the pathways. I stayed on the grass so my feet wouldn't *crinch-crunch* on the stone. Over the low wall to the terrace, and up to the glass doors.

All was quiet. I tried the door; it was locked. They hadn't come this way, then. I let out a breath of relief.

I was turning away, when my feet grated over something. I bent down and found a pile of dust, fine and oily under my fingers.

They *had* come this way!

I brushed the dust off my hands and reached back into my shirt collar for my lockpick wires, had them out in a moment, and snick-picked the lock. I slid in through the door and skiffed through the ballroom to the dark hallway beyond. No Shadows leaped out at me; all was silent.

Like a shadow myself, I raced through the

hallways and up the stairs to the duchess's chamber. A werelight should have burned in a sconce in the hallway, but it was dark.

On quiet feet I eased up to the duchess's door. My foot bumped up against something hard; I bent and felt cloth, a body, hardened into stone. Standing, I reached into my pocket and brought out the vial of sulfur emulsion; with my other hand I reached into my other pocket and scrabbled up a handful of saltpeter. With my teeth, I pulled out the stopper on the vial and spat it out. The door was open; I pushed it wider and edged in.

A candle had fallen to the floor, but it still burned; by its wavery light I saw a Shadow looming over the duchess, who lay across her bed, her arm hanging down, limp. A swathe of shadow went up, holding a shard of glittering stone.

'No!' I shouted.

The stone knife plunged down, stabbing the duchess. Then the Shadow whirled away from her and flowed over the bed toward me, ink-black smoke swirling around the glow of its eye.

I wasn't ready; it moved too fast. Its shadow-hands snaked around my neck; I gasped, and my breath came out as a puff of dust.

I dropped the vial. The glass shattered and the emulsion splashed across the floor. Then I dropped the saltpeter.

The blackpowder elements mingled.

The slow explosion started, with a muffled *whumph* and a cloud of grey smoke.

Across the room, the candle sputtered out and the room went dark. A heavy, stone feeling spread from my neck into my chest.

'Lothfalas!' I gasped. If the explosion didn't get the magic's attention, I was dead.

The magic heard the spell! From the floor, white-bright embers exploded, washing upward, swirling around the Shadow; it flinched away from me and, as the light burned through it, burst apart with a muffled puff into a cloud of black dust. Its glowing purple-black eye hung in the air.

I reached out and snatched the eye as it fell.

Then the wave of light flung me back against the wall and I went out.

I clutched the Shadow's eye, my fingers stiff as stone so I couldn't put it down. The eye struck spears of heavy numbness up my arm and into my bones. This must've been what Dee had felt just before he'd died.

I blinked away the blackness to find myself lying against the wall in the duchess's room.

Someone had come into the room; the candle was burning again, over by the duchess's bed.

My face was pressed into the floor; I felt the grittiness of dust under my cheek and smelled the smoke from the explosion. Through the hair hanging down into my eyes, I saw the dust-covered stone floor, a rug scuffed into a corner, shards of blackened glass from the vial of sulfur emulsion.

Feet in black leather shoes crunched over the dust, a cane tapped; I saw the hem of a magister's robe. Nevery. He crouched down and brushed the hair out of my eyes. I was too frozen into stone to speak.

'What happened here, my lad?' he said quietly. He rested his hand a moment on my stone forehead – I couldn't feel his fingers. Then he stood and strode to the door. 'Guards!' he called in his deep voice. He came back in, cast his eyes around, then crouched beside me again, fingering the black dust that lay all over me and the floor, picking up the shards of the vial. 'Ah, I see.' He swept up all the shards and put them into his coat pocket. Then he went over to the window and opened it.

Coming back over to me, he took off his robe and wrapped me in it, then – 'Quietly now, boy' – picked me up and carried me out to the hallway. He paused, looked around, and carried me farther, to the stairs, where he set me on a step, propped up against the wall.

A guard came rushing up the stairs. 'Yes, Magister?' he panted.

'A Shadow has attacked the duchess,' Nevery

answered. 'A guard is dead. Get Trammel up here at once.'

The guard hurried away, and after a minute two more guards raced up the stairs, followed by Trammel, holding a burning locus magicalicus in his hand.

'Stay here, lad,' Nevery said, and swept up the stairs with Trammel to the duchess's room.

I wasn't going anywhere.

After a minute, Captain Kerrn went by, taking the stairs two at a time, not noticing me.

I closed my eyes and hunched over, feeling my heavy, stone heart beating slowly inside my chest. My fingers felt frozen around the Shadow's eye, and heavy numbness flowed from it, up the bones of my arm.

A guard carrying a werelight lantern went by, followed by Rowan, who wore a sword in a scabbard belted around her waist over a white nightgown.

As she passed, Rowan saw me. She came and

crouched on the step below mine and peered into my face. 'What happened?'

My teeth were clenched by the stone spell. Even though I wasn't supposed to talk to her, I needed to tell her to go on upstairs, to check on her mother.

Rowan turned to the waiting guard. 'Mira, go find some blankets.'

The guard went off. Rowan sat on the step beside me. People passed us, hurrying up and down the stairs.

She took my hand. Not the one with the eye in it. 'You're cold.' She moved closer and put her arm around me; I rested my head against her shoulder. She felt so warm, like a glowing fire on a winter night. I closed my eyes.

Tap step step, I heard, coming down the stairs. 'How is he?' Nevery asked in a rumbly voice.

'He's very cold, sir,' Rowan said. Her breath on my cheek felt like candle flame.

Rowan's guard came up then with a blanket.

Rowan put it around me, then put her arms around me again.

'N-n-n—' I said, and shook my head. I couldn't move my mouth to speak. I wanted to tell Nevery about the Shadow's eye in my hand.

He leaned down and put his hand on my shoulder. 'It's all right, lad. Tell me later.'

'What happened?' Rowan asked.

'One of the Shadows attacked him,' Nevery said. 'Outside your mother's room.'

Outside? He'd found me inside, hadn't he?

Another set of footsteps came down the stairs and stopped a few steps above us.

'Lady Rowan!' said a deep voice. Her friend Argent, the one who gave her swordcraft lessons.

She looked up.

'Your mother, the duchess, was injured by the Shadows, Lady Rowan,' Argent said. 'Did you know?'

Rowan stood up abruptly. 'She was hurt? Will she be all right?' She gripped the hilt of her sword.

'Magister Trammel is with her,' Argent answered. 'I don't know if her injuries are serious. I will take you to her.'

As Argent and Rowan hurried away up the stairs, I heard Argent's voice ask, 'Who was *that*?'

I leaned against the wall, already missing Rowan's warmth.

'Can you walk, boy?' Nevery asked.

I nodded. The stone feeling was bad, but I could feel the Wellmet magic protecting me from the worst of it. Stiffly, I started climbing to my feet.

As I fell over, Nevery caught my arm and steadied me. 'Home to Heartsease,' Nevery said. 'I don't want Kerrn catching sight of you, boy, and asking awkward questions.'

Even if she did, I couldn't answer them.

CHAPTER 13

Nevery found Benet, and between them they got me home and wrapped in blankets in front of the fireplace in Nevery's study. Then Nevery did the dancing statue spell on me, and sent Benet down to the storeroom for more coal.

I sat in the chair and coughed up dust. Lady climbed into my lap and lay there like a warm pillow.

'Dust all over the floor,' Nevery said. He paced in front of the hearth. 'Glass shards. A smell of smoke. My guess is that you defeated a Shadow using a blackpowder explosive.'

I jerked out a nod.

'Boy, you set off a pyrotechnic device *in the duchess's chamber*. You may have saved her life, I grant you that, but no one can learn of this, especially not the magisters.' He shook his head. 'You do have a talent for getting yourself into trouble.'

I wasn't sure it was a talent.

Benet came in carrying a bucket of coal.

'All well?' Nevery asked him.

'Yes, sir. Before we left, Captain Kerrn said to tell you the Shadows retreated. One guard killed, six wounded.' He added more coal to the fire and nodded at me. 'He all right?'

'He will be,' Nevery said. 'Tea.'

Benet went out.

I wormed my arm out of the blankets, lifted my hand, still clenched around the Shadow's eye, and rested it on the table. One by one I pried my fingers open, and the stone rolled out of my hand and onto the table. It lay there glowing purple-black.

'What is that, boy?' Nevery asked, coming over to the table.

'Sh-sh-sh—' I said.

'Curse it,' he muttered. He reached for the eye.

'No—' I gasped out. It might turn him to stone, too.

Nevery paused, staring at me. 'Don't touch it, you mean, lad?'

I nodded.

'Very well,' Nevery said. He pulled the blankets over my arm again and sat down at the table, looking closely at the stone. 'Ah,' he said, glancing over at me. 'This was inside one of the Shadows, was it? The one you destroyed in the duchess's room?'

'Yss-s-s,' I said.

Benet came in with tea. He poured a cup and set it on the table before me. 'Manage that?' he asked.

I nodded and dragged my arm out of the blankets again. The teacup felt hot to my numb fingers. I leaned forward and took a drink, my teeth bumping the edge of the cup. The tea scorched a path down my throat, into my stomach. The stone inside me started to melt.

Benet sat down, tilted his chair back to lean against the wall, and picked up his knitting.

Nevery had fetched his magnifying glass from a shelf and leaned over the table, peering at the Shadow's eye. 'Hmmm,' he muttered. 'I've seen this before, haven't I?'

Setting down the glass, he went out of the room, up to his workroom, I guessed. In the silence, Benet's knitting needles went *clickety-ticky-tick*. After a few minutes Nevery came back.

'Look at this, boy.' He set a pot on the table.

It was about as big as his hand, made of smooth, red clay, with letters in black, swirling script along the side. 'I bought slowsilver in this pot. Hmmm.' He leaned back in his chair and stroked his beard. 'The same kind of writing, faint and fine, is etched on the eye. Slowsilver. The markings on the stone. I believe I know where the Shadows came from. They came from Desh, the desert city.'

Desh? Oh, how could I have been so stupid. The magic's spellword. It had the word *Desh* in it. The magic had known about the Shadows and where they had come from. But I'd been too stupid to understand it.

In the morning I woke up bundled in blankets, lying on the hearth, with Nevery nudging me with his foot. He added a shovelful of coal to the fire. 'Well, boy?'

I creaked up and leaned against the wall beside the hearth. Even with the blankets and the warm fire, I still felt the ache of cold stone in my bones. 'Better, Nevery,' I said. 'Is the duchess all right?' In my sleep, I'd dreamed the Shadow raising the stone knife, then plunging it down. And I'd dreamed Dee, too, with Shadow dust swirling around him.

'It is very early morning,' Nevery said. 'I haven't yet received a report from the Dawn Palace.'

I climbed up to my chair and sat at the table. The Shadow's eye was gone. In its place was a shiny, hand-sized puddle, as if a bit of night had spilled onto the scratched tabletop. I leaned closer to see.

Nevery joined me. 'Yes, it is odd, isn't it.' He held out his hand. 'Give me a lockpick wire.'

I reached into my pocket and brought one out and handed it to Nevery. He poked the end of the wire into the puddle. A black-dark bead stuck to the end of the wire; he tapped and it dropped onto the table, formed into a snail, and oozed back into the puddle. It left a sizzling trail of steam behind it.

'Slowsilver?' I asked.

Nevery shook his head. 'Something else, I think. Darksilver. Certainly it has magical properties.'

'How'd it make the Shadow come alive?'

'I suspect it was used to contain a bit of magic, which animated the Shadow and allowed it to carry out its orders.' He sat down. 'It is of very great concern.'

'It's from Desh?' I asked. I remembered Rowan telling me about Desh. A city built on sand and slowsilver mines, she'd said.

'Mmm,' Nevery said. 'I visited the city of Desh during my years of exile from Wellmet. The city is ruled by a sorcerer-king, Lord Jaggus. A very powerful wizard, though young.' He glanced at me from under his bushy eyebrows. 'His locus magicalicus is a large jewel stone.'

Like mine had been. 'D'you think Jaggus sent the Shadows?' I asked. The magic hadn't said the sorcerer-king's name, though, so maybe he hadn't.

'Possibly. I cannot imagine what he hopes to accomplish if he did. The Shadows are spies, perhaps, and are certainly murderers and assassins. Such aggression from one city toward another city; it makes no sense, and it is almost without precedent. There must be an explanation.' Nevery shook his head. 'I expect the duchess will send an envoy to Desh in order to discover the truth of the matter.'

Yes, she would. 'Nevery, I have to go with them. The magic warned me about Desh, and I think it wants me to go there.' I didn't want to leave the city, but if a group from Wellmet was going, I needed to go, too.

Nevery leaned back in his chair and pulled on the end of his beard. 'Hmmm. Perhaps,' he said.

He said *perhaps*, but he knew I was right.

Nevery was right about the duchess. She summoned him to the Dawn Palace the next day.

I went with him, putting on my black sweater and my apprentice robe, so they'd know I was a wizard.

As we walked up the front steps of the Dawn Palace, the guards at the door gave me a squinty-eyed look, but Nevery swept-stepped past them, me right behind him. We went up to the duchess's rooms. Outside the door, Trammel whispered to Nevery that the Shadow had struck the duchess with a stone blade that was spreading stone inside her, and that he should make his visit short.

'He should stay outside,' Trammel said, pointing at me. 'She doesn't need to be upset.'

'Well, boy?' Nevery asked, pulling at his beard.

I stayed outside; Nevery went in.

The guards outside the duchess's door glared at me, but I ignored them. I sat down with my back against the wall and closed my eyes. My neck felt numb where the Shadow had touched me.

Hearing hurrying footsteps, I opened my eyes.

Rowan, with a guard.

She stopped. 'Hello, Connwaer. You don't look much better than the last time I saw you. What are you doing here?'

I looked up at her. Her mother was right in the next room, and Kerrn's guards were an arm's length away; I wasn't going to talk to Rowan here.

Rowan waited for me to answer. 'Still not talking

to me, then?' she said after a few moments.

I shook my head.

'My mother,' she said with a sigh. 'I know.' She reached down with her hand; I took it, and she pulled me to my feet. 'You can come in with me,' she said.

But the guards wouldn't let me past the door. Rowan shrugged and went in, and I went back to sit against the wall and wait.

After a while, she came out. I got to my feet.

'Well,' Rowan said. 'You aren't talking to me, but I'm going to tell you my news anyway.' She smiled and her eyes sparkled. 'Conn, I'm being sent as an envoy to Desh to meet with the sorcerer-king, to try to find out if he sent the Shadows, and to bring back proof of it if he did.'

She was going to Desh? Drats. The duchess would never let me go if Rowan was going. I shook my head.

Rowan frowned. 'I'm leaving as soon as possible. Will you come see me off?'

I shook my head again. Why couldn't she just

stay here?

Rowan straightened, and suddenly she looked older, more like her mother. 'I thought you would be excited for me, but I can see that you're not. I am my mother's heir, Connwaer. One day I will be duchess. I've been trained for this; I've been taught diplomacy and policy and sword fighting for a reason. I will go to Desh and I will find out if they sent the Shadows, and I will make it right.' With one last glare, she turned with a swish of her skirts and stalked away down the hallway, followed by a guard.

The duchess's door opened and Nevery came out, looking grim. He put on his wide-brimmed hat. 'Come along, boy,' he said, sweep-stepping down the hallway. I followed.

In the tunnels on the way back to Heartsease, I asked him about his talk with the duchess.

He strode along, his cane going *tap tap* against the slippery slate floor of the tunnel, the blue glow from his locus magicalicus lighting our way. He paused to open a gate and we went through. 'We spoke about the envoyage to Desh,' he said at last. 'I suggested to the duchess that you be allowed to go along, but she would not allow it.'

Of course she wouldn't. So I'd be staying in Wellmet. That wasn't such a bad thing. Leaving Wellmet and the magic would be like walking away from a warm fire into a howling snowstorm; I didn't really want to do it.

'I wanted you out of the city,' Nevery said. 'It didn't escape my notice, boy, that you did magic using pyrotechnics in the duchess's chamber. The lothfalas spell, I assume?'

I nodded and kept quiet. He didn't look happy about it.

'The magisters are watching you,' he said. 'Captain Kerrn is watching you. They're both waiting for you to get into more trouble.'

'But Nevery, if I do pyrotechnics, I think I can talk to the magic,' I said.

Nevery stopped suddenly, bent, and stared

straight into my eyes. 'Listen, boy. Whether that is true or not, it is far too dangerous. You *must not* do any more pyrotechnic experiments.' He gripped my shoulder. 'Do you understand?'

I understood. But if I didn't do pyrotechnics, I was no use to the magic at all. I didn't answer Nevery. I didn't want to lie to him.

Rowan and the rest of her envoyage left the next day. Only one main road came to Wellmet, and it led from the Dawn Palace, through the city, and then east, to Desh eventually, I guessed.

Crowds of people, mostly from the Sunrise, had gathered along the street, standing under umbrellas in the drizzly rain, watching Rowan's envoyage leave. A few people cheered; a few more people worked the crowd, picking pockets.

The envoyage went past. First a group of guards in uniform, walking in quick-step through the puddles, then a wagon loaded with supplies with a waterproofed canvas spread over it, then a shabby carriage, full of servants, most likely. Then another carriage; I saw Nimble sitting inside. So they'd sent a wizard along. That was a good idea.

Then came Rowan. She rode a grey horse; its hooves clopped on the cobbled street. She wore dark green trousers, high boots, and an overcoat embroidered in green, and in the grey light her hair burned red, like flames. On one side of her rode Captain Kerrn in her green uniform; on the other rode her friend Argent on a fierce-looking black horse.

Rowan looked tall and noble and a little cold in the chilly wind. As she passed where I was standing, she looked down at me and then away, straight ahead, and rode on.

Rowan Forestal

My mother has asked me to write a journal, to note my observations. She says that writing things down will help me to 'articulate my experiences and thereby to understand them'. I suppose she is right about that. One thing I do not need to articulate any further is the fact that it was raining when we departed Wellmet, and continues to rain as I write this in my tent. The rain is articulated quite clearly in my wet coat, my wet boots, and the wet firewood that made the task of starting dinner rather difficult for our cook.

We need to hurry to Desh,, so I insisted that we put in a long day of travel right out of Wellmet. Argent looked very fine in his blue frock coat, mounted on tall Midnight, but I noticed that he climbed stiffly out of the saddle when we stopped to make camp. We will soon be travel hardened. The road to Desh

is a long one, and we must travel it swiftly.

Desh will be a challenge. The magister my mother assigned to accompany us, Nimble, thinks it is unlikely the sorcerer-king of Desh, Lord Jaggus, is responsible for the Shadow attacks. But Nimble strikes me as a fool. He makes me wish Conn had come with us. I have taken enough apprentice classes to suspect that Conn knows more about magic than all the other magisters combined. I don't know how he manages to make them, and my mother, and Captain Kerrn, so furious with him. Well, I suppose I am furious with him, too. It must be his particular talent.

In any case, this envoyage will be my chance to prove to my mother and her council that I have learned my lessons and am perfectly capable of carrying out the mission they have given me.

ᚻᚩᚹ ᚩᚱ ᚦᚩᚻᛁ ᚦᚩᚩᛉᚤ
ᚦᛁᚦᚣᚱᚩᚨ:

CHAPTER 14

In the middle of the afternoon, I waited until Nevery'd left for a magisters' meeting and Benet was scrubbing the kitchen, and snuck over to my workroom.

On the table were books, Nevery's treatise on pyrotechnics, dirty teacups,

an unlit candle, a saucer of sulfur emulsion, almost ready, and a cup full of saltpeter.

The black bird perched on the back of my chair; every once in a while it hopped onto my shoulder and peered down at what I was doing, keeping an eye on me for the magic.

I knew I wasn't going to find another locus magicalicus. But I also knew the magic wanted to tell me something, something about the Shadows and Desh, I guessed, and the only way I could hear that something was by doing pyrotechnics.

I cleaned off the glass rod I'd nicked from Nevery's workroom and stirred the emulsion in its saucer. The bird hopped down to the tabletop and poked its black beak into the saltpeter. 'Stop that, you,' I said, and pushed it away. It ruffled up its feathers, then flapped away to perch on the windowsill.

The blackpowder was just about ready.

Right.

It would just be a small explosion. Nevery wouldn't even notice it.

I cleared everything off the table, except for the saucer of sulfur emulsion. With the glass rod I gave it a stir, making the shiny black emulsion swirl around. Then I picked up the cup of saltpeter – the right amount, according to the ratios Embre had written out. Taking a deep breath, I dumped the saltpeter into the saucer.

I took a step back from the table.

The saltpeter soaked down into the swirling emulsion. It crackled; bits of light sparked on the surface; smoke gathered around the edge of the saucer.

On the table and on the floor, tiny motes of dust started jumping around like fleas on a dog. The walls shivered. Glass vials and bottles rattled off the shelves and shattered on the floor. The dragon in the picture on the wall seemed to writhe in a cloud of smoke, winking at me with its red eye.

With a *whumph*, fire and smoke billowed from the saucer. Bolts of white light flashed from one end of the room to the other; books floated from the shelves; papers whirled around. The walls vibrated; the ceiling cracked across. Under my feet, the floor heaved. The magic had to listen. These weren't the right spellwords, but I had to make it hear. I took a deep breath. '*Tell me*,' I shouted at the magic. '*I can't go to Desh. What d'you want me to do now?*'

As the word left my mouth, I was hurled backward. I should have slammed into the workroom wall, but I didn't. Sparks spun in front of my eyes; I fell through the air; huge blocks of stone hurtled past me, arrows of light shot upward then away. I blinked, and saw the black bird, its wings spread wide, swoop around me once and then tumble away, into the light.

The magic spoke. Like a giant hand it surrounded me. Its voice vibrated in my bones and in my teeth like deep music. It said the same thing it had said before, but this time building from a low note up to a high shriek, three times, faster and faster, *Damrodellodesseldeshellarhionvarliarden-liesh – desh*desh*desh*!

The magic held me for another moment. Then it dropped me, and I fell.

CHAPTER 15

Down I crashed, lashed by twigs, bouncing off branches, until a bigger branch caught me and held me like a big bony hand.

In the fall, my arm bone popped out of its shoulder joint; the pain of it speared into me. I blinked red flashes out of my eyes. I was in the courtyard tree. My apprentice's robe was caught on a twig just above me, my body and legs were held by a spreading branch, and my head hung out over open space. I moved, my shoulder sending jabs of pain into me, and the branches holding me shifted. I kept still, trying not to breathe, because my breaths hurt going in. I closed my eyes.

A fluttering noise came from just above, then *grawwwk*. I opened my eyes. The black bird had perched on a branch above me and pecked at my apprentice's robe. *Peck peck peck*. The cloth twitched off the twig; my weight shifted, and the branches let me go.

I bounced off another branch and splatted onto the cobblestones.

My shoulder popped back in. And I went out.

I woke up in a bed, my bones aching. White plaster walls, a tiled floor, and a high window; next to my bed, a table with a brown bottle and spoon on it. The medicos, I guessed.

The door opened. Nevery came in. His face was grim, like it was chipped out of stone. He stood at the end of my bed and looked down at me. In his black suit, with his stone face, he was a stern, black column. He opened his mouth, about to speak, then he clenched his teeth, turned, and left the room.

Oh, no.

Slowly, creaking, I sat up and swung my feet off the bed. I was still wearing my clothes, but my feet were bare. My head hurt. My shoulder ached. My ribs on the same side hurt even worse.

The door opened again and Trammel came in, wearing a white apron with blood spattered across the front of it.

I stared at the blood spatters. They were dark red against the snowy white. Nevery stepped into the room and closed the door behind him.

'Stand up,' Trammel ordered.

I stood slowly up. The tiled floor felt cold under my bare feet.

'Raise your arms,' Trammel said.

Ow. My ribs twinged. The shoulder that had popped out of its joint only let me raise that arm halfway.

'Does this hurt?' Trammel asked, pressing against my side.

Like being stabbed with a knife. I nodded.

'And when you breathe in?'

I nodded again.

'Hmmm,' Trammel said. He turned and put his back to me, talking only to Nevery. 'Dislocated shoulder, but it's back in its socket. Cracked ribs. Keep him quiet for ten days. If you can. Now I have another patient to see to.'

Trammel left the room, and without speaking to me, Nevery followed him out.

Under my sore ribs, my heart was pounding. My pyrotechnic experiment had gone wrong, clear as clear, and Nevery was too angry even to speak to me.

I found my boots and socks under the bed. Aching as I bent over, I put them on. I headed for the door and peeked out. The medicos hallway was empty.

Every step sent a jolt of pain through my ribs and into my shoulder, so I walked carefully out of my room and down the hallway. The door of the next room was open a crack. I peeked in.

Nevery was there, sitting beside a bed, his head in his hands. Trammel stood beside him, holding a grimoire and his locus magicalicus, doing a healing spell.

Lying in the bed was Benet.

Benet?

His eyes were closed, his skin was paper white, and his head was wrapped in bandages; a patch of blood had seeped through in one spot. One of his arms lay on top of the covers, splinted and bandaged.

I pushed the door open.

Nevery looked up. When he saw me, he scowled. He got slowly to his feet and pointed at the door. 'Get out.' I had never heard him so angry.

His words hit me like a blow across the face. I stumbled back and leaned against the wall outside.

Benet in the bed, hurt, maybe dying.

What had happened?

After a moment Nevery came out into the hallway, closing the door behind him. His face looked like thunder and lightning ready to strike.

My heart shivered in my chest. Benet with his head wrapped up in bandages . . . 'Is he going to be all right?' I whispered.

'I don't know. Trammel has spell-knit his bones, but he doesn't know.' Nevery clenched his hands into fists. I expected him to hit me, but instead he turned and stalked away. Then he whirled and came back and shouted, 'His skull is broken, curse it!'

My stomach felt cold, as if I'd swallowed a misery eel. I stared up at him. Was it my fault?

The door behind him opened and Trammel poked his head out. 'Quiet, please,' he said in a sharp voice. 'He must not be disturbed.'

Nevery nodded, then turned back to me. This time he whispered, but it was worse than shouting. 'Go to Heartsease and see what you have done.'

I went.

It took me a while to make my way through the tunnels and back to Heartsease. The ache from my ribs and shoulder jabbed through me with every step and every breath, so after every gate I went through I had to stop and lean against the wall with my eyes closed.

At the Heartsease stairs I stopped to rest, hunched over on the step with my arms wrapped around my ribs, trying to hold them together so they would stop hurting. It didn't work.

Trying to take small breaths, I got to my feet again and climbed the stairs. At the top I stopped.

Across the courtyard, Heartsease lay in smoking ruins. My workroom was gone, as if it had been scraped off the island, leaving nothing behind, just bare rock. And the rest of the building, Nevery's study, the kitchen, the storeroom, my attic room – nothing but tumbled piles of bricks, scorched and splintered wood, chunks of sand-coloured stone. Smoke spiralled up from the shattered walls where the storeroom had been.

Benet had been in there when I'd done the pyrotechnics. The magic had protected me well enough, but it hadn't protected him.

While I'd sat on the steps the sun had set; the air smelled of the muddy river and of smoke. From the east, fingers of darkness reached across the sky.

Inside me something strange was happening. Since becoming Nevery's apprentice I'd built the thought of a home where I was safe and had enough to eat and a place to sleep. And inside me the idea of home crumbled into smoking ruins. It left behind a gaping, dark, empty space. Our home. My fault.

Benet. My fault.

The darkness inside me joined with the night outside, and everything went black.

I woke up in the morning lying under the tree in the courtyard. When I opened my eyes I saw the black bird perched on my chest. It cocked its head and blinked one of its yellow eyes at me.

'G'morning,' I croaked.

Krrrrr, it said.

I let my head fall sideways, to look toward Heartsease. The tumbled stones were rosy in the early morning light.

In the grey shadows something moved, then crossed the courtyard toward where I lay.

Lady, the cat. A little of the dark emptiness inside me went away. She padded up and sat down, eyeing the black bird. It hop-flapped down to my feet and perched there, ruffling its feathers. Lady came and put her paws on my arm, purring.

I started lifting my hand to pet her, then let it fall again. Ow. All the pain from the day before had stiffened and set into my bones; I felt like an old man who'd been run over by a cart. I would just lie here for a while, I decided. I closed my eyes.

From down in the tunnel came the sound of the Heartsease gate opening and closing, then heavy footsteps coming up the stairs and *step step tapping* across the cobbles. I opened my eyes.

Nevery.

As he came nearer, I edged up so I was sitting against the tree trunk. The black bird flew up to perch in a branch over my head.

Nevery stopped beside me, looking out over the ruin of Heartsease. He held a canvas knapsack. 'He is no better this morning,' he said. His voice was flat and cold.

I wrapped my arms around myself, then got slowly to my feet.

Nevery dropped the knapsack. I expected him to shout at me some more, but he didn't say anything, just stared frowningly at me.

Across the courtyard, the piles of broken stone

smoked. A chilly breeze blew off the river and across the ruins, bringing with it ash and dust.

He'd told me not to do pyrotechnics, and I had.

'I'm sorry, Nevery,' I whispered. 'I'm so sorry.'

Then he shook his head. 'It is too late for that. Now you must do what you must.' He turned and *step-step-tapped* away toward the ruins. Lady followed him. Clouds gathered across the river, over the Sunrise. Far away, thunder grumbled and rain began to fall.

I picked up the knapsack and looked in. Food wrapped in brown paper packages. Plenty of food.

I took a deep, shuddery breath, and my ribs stabbed me in the side.

Nevery would never forgive me for destroying Heartsease. *Never*. It was his home; he'd grown up here. And Benet. He wouldn't forgive me for that, either. He shouldn't.

My hands were shaking; I clenched them around the straps of the knapsack. Clear as clear, the magic had told me what it wanted. It wanted me out of Wellmet; it wanted me to go to Desh. I should have gone before, even without the envoyage. Staying here had been stupid.

And now look what I'd done. The magisters and duchess would meet, and they would issue an order of exile. Nevery had warned me this would happen; he wouldn't try to change their minds. He wanted me to go. The magic wanted me to go.

So I would leave Wellmet.

I'd never left the city before. As I headed slowly toward the eastern road, where I'd watched Rowan leave a few days before, my heart felt heavier than a bucket full of rocks. A grizzle-grey rain fell.

The black bird came along with me, flying ahead and perching on something, and watching me creak-walk along the puddled streets with the knapsack on my back.

At the edge of the city the houses ended, and the cobbled street ended, and a rutted muddy road began, leading down a steep hill and into a dark forest. I stood with my feet half on cobbled street and half on road. The bird flapped to a low stone wall beside the road and perched there, cocking its head to fix me with its yellow eye.

Right. Time to go. I gritted my teeth against the sadness and lifted my foot to step forward, out of Wellmet.

As I brought my foot down, the magic of the city washed up like a giant hand, pushing me from behind, and down I fell. I tumbled, my ribs stabbing me, all the way to the bottom of the hill.

I lay there covered with mud, and looked up at the grey sky. Raindrops fell onto my face. My ribs ached. I didn't feel like moving. What if I just lay there and didn't go to Desh at all?

I lay there for a while. The mud soaked into my clothes. The rain came down harder. I got colder. And hungrier.

This was stupid. I didn't have a home anymore, so I'd have to go on. Creaking, I sat up and wiped the rain out of my eyes, then stood. The knapsack had fallen off me a few paces away, so I trudged over, picked it up, and put it on.

I looked back up the hill. The black bird sat in the middle of the road, where the cobbled street began. It hopped up, fluttering its wings, then settled down again. *Awwwwwk*, it called. *Go away*.

'All right, I'm going,' I said, and I turned my back on the city and walked away.

CHAPTER 16

At the bottom of the hill, the forest began. In the grey rainy light the road looked like a tunnel leading into darkness. Brown-leafed bushes crowded up to the road, and over them loomed trees with knobbly bark, twisted branches, and dark leaves. Vines hung down between the trees, and a milky fog lay close to the ground. The air smelled of rotting leaves and mould. I walked slowly along, my boots muddy, the pack heavy.

As I left Wellmet I felt the magic of the city getting farther away. It was like walking away from a warm fire. As the magic faded into the distance, the rain felt colder; my stomach felt emptier; the ache from my ribs and shoulder got worse with every step.

The tunnel through the trees grew darker and darker until I realized that I could barely see the road under my feet. Time to stop. I walked along the edge of the road until I found a good place to sleep – a bush full of brown, rustly leaves, with a dry spot underneath, out of the rain. I crawled in, dragging the knapsack behind me, and crouched, leaves rustling around my head and twigs poking into my back.

I opened the knapsack to see what Nevery had packed. A knife in a leather sheath. A packet of biscuits, one of cooked bacon, three apples, five cooked potatoes, a lump of cheese wrapped in waxed paper, and a canteen filled with water.

The night had grown completely dark. It was never this dark in Wellmet; even on a rainy night, the werelights from the Sunrise reflected off the clouds and made the night glow pink.

By touch, I brought out a biscuit and two pieces of bacon, made a sandwich, and took a bite.

What was Nevery doing right now? I closed my eyes. He was across the table from me. He was eating chicken pie and pointing at me with his fork, telling me not to wipe my face on my sleeve. *Use your napkin, boy*, he said. Later we would go up to the study and I would ask him about the papers he'd written on pyrotechnics, the ones I'd nicked from his study. Lady would curl up on my lap and purr. Benet would bring up tea and then sit with his chair tilted back against the wall, knitting.

I chewed at my bite of biscuit and bacon and

finally swallowed it down, but the lump of sadness in my throat wouldn't let me eat any more. Carefully, I wrapped up the biscuit again and put it back in the knapsack.

I lay down to sleep, using the knapsack as a pillow, shivering because my clothes were damp. The leaves of the bush rustled, and drops of rain pattered down nearby. My eyes stayed open, and I stared at the black night. High above, the wind blew in the treetops. It sounded like somebody sighing, far, far away, *alas, alas, alas*.

The next morning when I woke up, I felt awful. Not because I was tired, but because of something else. The inside of my neck hurt and my head felt watery and strange, like it was going to fall off and roll across the ground.

I knew what it was. I was sick with a cold. In Wellmet I'd never gotten sick, ever, because the magic had protected me. But it couldn't protect me way out here on the road to Desh.

I sneezed and crawled out from under my bush. The rain kept up all day, just a drizzle that made everything damp but not wet. Wellmet's magic felt very far away, just a warm spark in the distance. My cold got worse, my head aching with every step. My shoulder hurt. The road grew muddier. It led on, straight through the trees. If I followed it, I reckoned, and walked fast, I would catch up with Rowan and her envoyage. I wasn't sure Rowan would let me join her, but one way or another I would get to Desh.

I walked all the rest of the day, sneezing and sniffling and wiping my nose on my sleeve. Finally the night crept through the trees. Like the night before, I found a bush to sleep under, this one farther away from the road.

I couldn't feel the magic at all anymore, not even a glimmer in the distance. My ribs aching, my head aching, I crawled into the bush; even under its rustly leaves the ground was wet, but I wasn't going to find anywhere drier. I'd spent wetter nights in the Twilight. After eating a potato and some cheese and telling my growling stomach it wasn't getting any more, I lay down to sleep.

The night was empty, and darker than a cellar with the door closed. Nearby I heard rustling, twigs cracking, scurryings. What was it? Little animals, I guessed. Maybe rats. There were always plenty of rats around in the Twilight. Sometimes, if you slept in a dark cellar, they'd creep out during the night and nibble at your hair.

My eyes fell shut and I went to sleep.

Went to survey damage. Heartsease utterly destroyed. Nothing salvageable. Grimoire lost, curse it. Will have to rebuild from ground up.

Benet has not yet woken. Trammel grows more worried, fears his brain injured when skull was cracked.

Met with magisters. Discussed Connwaer's exile. Order of exile issued. Discussed Shadows. Magisters grow more worried every day.

Staying in Brumbee's apartments in academicos. Uncomfortable; don't like it. Can't sleep. I fear something is deeply wrong, more than we know.

·⊼́ó⏦ ⏃̊◌̊ठ:

CHAPTER 17

Four more days of walking as fast as I could through the mud with my sore throat and my ribs aching, and sleeping under bushes. I ran out of food on the third morning, after eating the last crumbs of cheese and a half potato for breakfast. Living with Nevery and Benet,

I'd forgotten what it was like to be hungry. My stomach felt hollow, and by the next morning my head did, too.

Eventually the night came on. Instead of looking for a bush to sleep under, I kept walking, *plod*, *plod*, *plod* down the road in the dark.

I caught up with the envoyage the next day. It was still early morning; the sky overhead was dark grey, and a light rain drifted down. My cold was a little better, but my head spun, from hunger and from relief. I stopped to look over the camp. It was a cluster of white canvas tents in a grassy clearing just off the road. A couple of fire pits were scattered around; the horses were tethered together and the wagon and the carriages were pulled up next to the road. I saw a few people, guards and servants, carrying firewood and buckets of water.

Rowan was in the biggest tent, I reckoned. I walked into the camp.

I'd only taken three steps when somebody grabbed me and jerked me off my feet. She spun me to face her.

Kerrn, with one of her guards. Drats.

'Rowan!' I shouted. Kerrn clapped her hand over my mouth. I struggled, my ribs twinging, but she and the other guard picked me up and carried me into another tent, at the other end of the camp. They set me on my feet, and I made a dive for the tent flap to get outside.

'Ro—' I got out, and then Kerrn had me by the collar and twisted, choking me.

The tent had a central pole holding it up. Kerrn slammed me up against it; she searched me, and came up with my knife. She held it up in her other hand. 'Well, well. What are you doing here, little thief?' she asked. She twisted my collar tighter and thumped me back against the post.

I gasped for breath. Dark spots flashed in front of my eyes.

Someone else came into the tent, ducking

under the flap and standing just inside. He said something, and Kerrn let me go.

I bent over, holding on to the pole, catching my breath.

'We caught this thief sneaking into the camp with a knife,' Kerrn said.

'Ah, I see. But Captain, I believe Lady Rowan knows him,' said the man. I looked up. Argent. Rowan's friend, the one who taught her sword-craft lessons.

'I need to talk to her,' I said to him. 'And I wasn't sneaking,' I said to Kerrn.

'Be quiet, thief,' Kerrn growled.

Argent was tall, looked a few years older than Rowan, and had blond hair neatly combed, blue eyes, and a long nose for looking down. He looked down it at me and snorted. 'I suppose she will have to see him, Captain.' He turned to leave.

Kerrn grabbed my shoulder – my bad shoulder, ow – and pushed me after Argent; I followed him out of the tent, trying not to stumble.

Dragging me by the collar, Kerrn brought me to a fire, where one of the servants stirred a pot of something that smelled delicious. Porridge, I guessed. With raisins in it.

Argent ducked into the big tent nearby, and after a short while came out again with Rowan.

She saw me and raised her eyebrows. 'Well, Connwaer,' she said.

'Hello, Ro,' I said.

'So you'll talk to me now, will you?'

I nodded.

Kerrn still held me by the collar.

'Captain, you may release him,' Rowan said.

'Are you sure, Lady Rowan?' she asked. 'We caught him sneaking into camp with a knife.'

'I am quite sure,' Rowan said. She was annoyed, I could tell. Kerrn let me go.

At the fire, the servant started dishing out bowls full of the porridge. They were frying bacon, too. My stomach growled.

'Are you listening, Conn?' Rowan said.

I turned back to her. 'Sorry,' I said.

'I asked why you are here.'

I opened my mouth to tell her, but the pyro-technics, Heartease, Benet, Nevery – it was too much to explain. I shook my head.

Rowan's eyes widened; she could see that I was in trouble. 'All right. You're coming with us, though?'

I nodded. Yes, all the way to Desh. And what I would do once I got there, I wasn't sure.

Rowan Forestal

This morning Conn walked into camp.

My mother told me I would face challenges on this journey, and that I must 'assert my leadership.' One challenge is to decide what to do with Conn. I asked Magister Nimble to take him on as an apprentice until we return to Wellmet. Nimble said, <u>Absolutely not</u>. Meanwhile Captain Kerrn wants to arrest Conn – for our own protection. She warns very darkly that Conn will land us in trouble unless he is chained up.

Then during our ride, Argent asked if he could have Conn as his servant. I suppose Argent's idea is better than turning Conn over to Captain Kerrn. Knowing Conn, he will not like being a servant, but he must be given something to do or he will get into trouble. Argent will keep him out of Kerrn's way.

We don't have time for these distractions. A broken

carriage wheel slowed us down yesterday, and I was half-tempted to leave it behind. We must get to Desh as soon as possible. While we are on the road, who knows what terrible things are happening back home in Wellmet. I cannot get Conn to speak of them. I am worried about my mother, too, and the wound she suffered. Magister Trammel said she was improving, but she seemed so weak and pale before we left.

CHAPTER 18

The first thing I did was steal my knife back from Captain Kerrn. And I nicked one of her knives, too, because I'd be better off with two. I hid them in Rowan's bags, so when Kerrn grabbed me and searched me she didn't find them.

As Kerrn stalked away with steam coming out of her ears, Rowan came up to me. We'd been travelling all day; after eating a big breakfast I'd taken a long nap in the cart with the baggage, resting my shoulder and ribs, which were still sore. Rowan had ridden her horse alongside Argent and Kerrn. Now we'd camped in a forest clearing.

'Conn,' Rowan said, shaking her head, 'you're going to get into trouble. You need something to keep you busy.'

No, I didn't. I had plenty to do, just travelling to Desh.

'And as the leader of this envoyage, I've decided what that something will be.' Rowan folded her arms and gave me her sly, slanting look. 'Several somethings, actually.'

I narrowed my eyes.

'You don't need to glare at me, my lad,' she said. 'The first thing is, I want you to write to Magister Nevery and tell him you've joined us and that you are well.'

I shook my head. If Nevery got a letter from me, he'd just throw it in the fire.

'The second thing,' Rowan said, 'is that you will serve Argent.'

'No,' I said.

'No one else will take you on, Conn. It's Argent or nobody.'

'Nobody, then,' I said.

Rowan shook her head. 'Argent is a very good friend; he will treat you well, don't worry.' Argent himself was passing by, and she called to him. He set down the horse's saddle he was carrying and came over.

'Yes, Lady Rowan?' he said, with a little bow of his head. He ignored me standing there.

Rowan smiled at him. 'Argent, this is Conn, your new servant.'

'I didn't agree to this, Ro,' I said.

'Hush,' she answered. 'It's for your own good. You will serve him until we get home to Wellmet.'

Except that I wasn't going home to Wellmet. I knew this, but every time I thought of it a new misery eel hatched in my stomach. Then I thought about Benet and a whole nest of eels hatched. I kept quiet.

Argent bowed. 'Thank you, Lady Rowan.'

'I think you will get along well,' Rowan said, 'if you give each other a chance.' She pointed at me. 'Conn, if you want to travel with us, you must make yourself useful.'

Argent bowed again, and Rowan walked away, smiling.

For just a moment I hated her.

Argent looked down his long nose at me. 'It is quite clear to me that you are not a proper servant. You are scruffy, and Captain Kerrn says you are a thief, and you talk like a gutterboy.'

Because I *was* a thief and a gutterboy. Stupid Argent. He'd be scruffy, too, if he'd slept under a bush for the past six nights. 'I am *not* your servant, Argent,' I said.

His lip curled. 'Apparently you are. The alternative is that.' He pointed at the forest. I'd have to leave the envoyage, he meant, unless I served him. Drats.

'I feel it is my duty to teach you better manners. To begin, boy, you will refer to me as *Sir* Argent.'

'And you will refer to me as Conn,' I said. Only Nevery called me *boy*.

That night I was sleeping under a tree at the edge of the camp, wrapped up in a blanket. It was either that or share a tent with Argent, and he snored.

In the middle of the night, something woke me up.

The clouds had thinned and the moon hung behind them. It was quiet. No leaves rustled, no twigs snapped, no wind blew in the treetops. The silence pushed against my ears.

From far away, I heard a rushing sound, getting closer, coming along the road, heading toward Wellmet. Before it came a wave of dusty air.

Coughing, wrapping the blanket tightly around me, I crawled over wet grass toward the edge of the road.

I crouched behind a tree trunk and peered out. Overhead, the trees swayed, the leaves tearing off their branches and whirling away in the wind.

Along the road, they came. As I ducked back behind the tree to hide, I caught a glimpse of purple-black light and the fluttering of black shadows, and I heard the rushing of them coming closer.

The rushing suddenly stopped and the night grew still as still. The air felt heavy, like in a Wellmet cellar. Around me I heard *tink, tink* and then patterings on the ground. Leaves were turning to stone and falling off the trees. From the road came a purple-black glow.

Shadows.

I wrapped my arms around myself and put my head down on my knees.

From the camp came a shout. First one of the

189

guards – ''Ware!' – then Kerrn calling the rest of the guards to arms. I heard the sound of swords being drawn and Nimble shrieking out the lothfalas spell, but there was no magic here so the spell didn't work. The camp stayed dark.

'At the road!' Rowan shouted from over by her tent.

With a sudden *whoosh,* the Shadows moved. The wind shrieked. The trees thrashed. Then silence.

They were gone, away to Wellmet.

CHAPTER 19

nother day of trudge-travel through the forest. Everyone was twitchy because of the Shadows, worrying that they were headed to Wellmet, or that we'd be attacked if they came back.

In the late afternoon, when we'd set up camp, Rowan led Argent and me to a smaller clearing in the forest. She put her hands on her hips and looked around. 'We need to be ready if those Shadows return. Argent?'

He nodded. 'Fetch the practice swords,' he said to me. 'They're in the baggage.'

'Fetch them yourself,' I said. My bones ached from walking all day.

He glanced at Rowan, who raised her eyebrows. 'Do as he asks, Conn,' Rowan said. She leaned down to touch her toes, then stood and stretched.

I didn't say anything. But I went and fetched the practice swords, which were made out of wood with leather-wrapped handles. As I was pulling them out of a bag, Kerrn grabbed my arm.

'What are you doing, thief?' she asked.

I showed her the swords. 'Rowan and Argent are going to practice.'

'Ah!' she said, and let me go. She followed

me to the clearing.

I handed Rowan the swords, and she gave one to Argent.

I went across the clearing and leaned against a tree, watching her shake out her arms, getting ready. Sword practice. I'd never seen anyone practise before. I'd seen fights, sometimes with swords, but more often with broken bottles and knives or truncheons, and somebody always got hurt. This might be interesting.

'All right,' Rowan said. 'Ready?' She bounced on the balls of her feet.

'Ready,' Argent said.

'Commence.' She took up a ready position and tapped his wooden blade. He tapped back, and they fell into a regular pattern. 'Quarters,' she said, and the pattern changed. 'To eight,' and it changed again.

It seemed a very polite way to fight. I slid down the tree trunk and sat on the damp, grassy ground. *Tap, tip, tap* went their blades. I nibbled on grass stems and watched their back and forth.

'Enough!' Rowan said after a while. She was panting and smiling; her red hair was tangled up like flickering flames. She glanced over at me. 'Now it's your turn, Conn.'

Me? I spat out the grass I was chewing and scrambled to my feet.

Rowan handed me her practice sword.

'I don't know how to use this,' I said. The sword was heavy, and the grip felt warm and sweaty-damp. I gripped it tightly.

'Even wizards need to know swordcraft.' She motioned for Argent to come closer. 'We've encountered Shadows once already. Argent can teach you to take care of yourself in a fight.'

But I already knew how to take care of myself in a fight.

'We'll start with the very basics,' Rowan said. 'Stand at the ready.'

Across from me, Argent showed his teeth, raised his sword, and crouched. He looked very ready. Ready to slaughter me.

Rowan frowned at him. 'Just the first position.'

Argent relaxed, but just a little. I raised my sword. My sore shoulder told me to lower my hand, and my ribs twinged.

'Tell the thief to keep his guard up,' Kerrn called from the edge of the clearing.

'Keep your guard up, Conn,' Rowan said, stepping back. 'And loosen your shoulders. Now, engage.'

Argent's blade tapped mine. I tapped his back. He tapped again, more firmly, and I felt the vibration in my fingers, up my arm, and into my sore shoulder. His eyes narrowed and he tapped again, hard enough to push my blade out of the way, then reached out with the point of his sword. I flinched and felt the blow brush past my sore ribs. He went into the ready position again and advanced toward me. I backed away.

'Put your blade up again,' Rowan said.

'This is a bad idea, Ro,' I said. I switched the

sword to my other hand, on the side without the sore shoulder.

'No, this is serious,' she said. 'Knowing how to wield a sword could save your life.'

No it wouldn't. Because I wouldn't be carrying a sword in the first place.

Argent advanced toward me again, moving smoothly, the point of his sword steady. He was, I realized, a very good swordsman; he'd been practising nicely with Rowan, but he planned something else for me.

His blade tapped mine. As before, I tapped back. *Tap-tap. Tip-tap.* And again he lunged toward me, only this time I was too slow. The blunt tip of his sword slammed into my shoulder, right where it hurt most; I dropped my sword and stumbled backward. Ow. I rubbed the knot of pain.

'You'd be dead,' Argent said, eyes narrowed.

Rowan, who'd been following us closely, picked up the sword and handed it to me. 'And again,' she said.

No, not again.

This time, after the *tap-tap* and *tip-tap*, when Argent attacked, I was ready.

He batted my sword aside and came at me like a hurled spear, blade extended toward my heart.

I scrambled out of the way and threw my wooden sword as hard as I could at his head. Then I ducked his swung blade, and flung myself into a bush at the edge of the clearing. Twigs snagged my sweater and leaves brushed against my face as I crawled farther in.

Leaves rustled; Argent poked his sword into the bush. 'Come out of there!' he shouted.

Not likely.

He poked again, closer, then again. His wooden blade plunged into the leaves beside my head; I grabbed its blunt tip with both hands and pulled hard.

Argent shouted as he overbalanced and fell into the bush. Cursing and thrashing, he climbed out again.

I crouched, gripping his sword. My shoulder throbbed where he'd hit me, and my ribs ached.

All was silent for a few moments. I shifted to get clear of a branch that was jabbing me in the leg.

Then I heard Rowan's voice talking quietly to Argent.

'All right,' he grumbled.

She spoke more loudly, and I could tell she was trying not to laugh. 'You can come out now, Conn.'

She'd calmed him down, then. Pushing branches out of the way, I crawled out and got to my feet.

Argent stood with his arms folded, glaring. He had a bloody scratch on his face and leaves in his hair. I glared back at him. My shoulder hurt. Rowan, hiding a grin, stepped between us. 'The sword, Connwaer?' she said, holding out her hand. At the edge of the clearing, Kerrn was smiling.

I realized I was holding the sword tightly, ready to throw it at Argent if he went for me again.

Loosening my grip, I handed it to her. She, in turn, handed it to Argent.

'Thank you, Lady Rowan,' he said, still glaring at me.

'We'll have to try this again tomorrow,' Rowan said.

Argent and I turned to stare at her.

She smiled. 'I think you can both learn a lot from each other.'

CHAPTER 20

Another day of travelling. As we went along, me walking at the back as usual, the trees grew smaller and farther apart until the road came out of the forest into a wide plain with waving, high brown grasses as far as I could see.

Birds swooped through the air and perched on the bending grass to sing; bugs in the grasses went *chrrr-chrrr-chrrr*. The clouds had cleared off and the sky arched overhead and down to the edge of the land all around, like a wide, blue bowl. I kept stopping to look over my shoulder to see if something was sneaking up on me through the high grass. It was too wide open, with no trees and no buildings.

After dinner I lugged buckets of water from a stream for Argent's horse, and helped set up our tent and bedrolls, and washed dishes, and cleaned every speck of dust off of Argent's horse's saddle. Then, more swordcraft lessons.

We had the lesson in a patch of trampled-down grass, with Kerrn and a few of her guards watching and Rowan telling us what to do.

After Rowan and Kerrn had shouted at me to keep my guard up, and Argent had bashed me in the ribs five times, they decided that I'd lost enough fluff, so I got to collect the swords and put them away, fetch more water for the horses, and clean Argent's boots. Then I had to write the letter to Nevery, Rowan said.

We sat on folding chairs at a camp table set up in Rowan's tent with a candle and a bottle of ink between us. She squinted down at her paper, writing fast, in neat, straight lines, an entry in her journal.

I sat there with the blank page in front of me.

'Write, Connwaer,' Rowan said without looking up.

All right. I dipped the metal nib of the pen into the ink.

Dear Nevery . . .

No, I couldn't start my letter that way. I tore off the written-on strip of paper from the top of the page and started again.

To Master Nevery . . .

Stupid. Now that I'd left Wellmet, he wasn't my master, was he? I tore off more paper and tried again.

To Nevery ...

I looked it over. A good beginning. But my handwriting was terrible. Nevery hated it when he couldn't read my writing. I tore off another strip of paper.

Inkblots. Messy. Tear off paper, start again.

To Nevery, I printed. What next?

Drats. I'd run out of paper.

I put down the pen, leaned back in my chair, and looked up at the curving white ceiling of the tent. Candlelight flickered; Rowan's pen went *scritch-scritch*. Then it stopped.

'You're not making much progress,' she said, putting a new piece of paper on the table in front of me.

I would have shrugged, but shrugging hurt my shoulder.

'I'm sure Magister Nevery would like to receive a letter from you, Conn. Otherwise he'll worry.'

I wasn't sure of that at all.

After a few silent moments Rowan went back to her journal, and I watched the shadows flicker across the tent ceiling.

'Get on with it,' Rowan said, turning her paper over.

All right. I picked up my pen and got to work.

To Nevery,

Rowan asked me to write to you. I joined her envoyage to Desh. I am very well.

I hope Benet is better. Please say hello to him for me and tell him I miss him and I am very well.

I am very sorry, Nevery.

From,

Connwaer

We went on across the grassy plain, under the blue-bowl sky.

When we left the forest, we left the rain behind. The air was dry here, and warmer. The road was two narrow wagon-wheel tracks with a strip of grass in the middle.

In the middle of the day Kerrn got off her horse by a wagon and handed the driver the reins. Then, as the wagon and her horse went on, she waited for me to catch up. She held her sword, unsheathed.

I stopped in the middle of the road. What was Kerrn up to? She wasn't going to attack me with the sword, was she? Or grab me and search me? I had my knife in my coat pocket and her knife hidden in my boot. I wiped dust out of my eyes with my sleeve and got ready to run.

'You should not allow Sir Argent to riposte,' she said.

Riposte?

'When he parried your blade and touched you with his. A riposte.'

Oh. She wanted to talk about swordcraft.

'I will show you something.' She held up the sword; it glinted in the sunlight. '"Keep your guard up" means you must position your arm and hand like this.' Standing on one of the hard-packed wagon-wheel tracks, she showed me.

I nodded. Why was she telling me this?

'Now you,' she said. She handed me her sword. It was heavier than the wooden ones we used in practice.

I stood as she'd shown me, arm up. The dust from the wagon and horses settled.

'I noticed, at the first lesson, that you started with your right hand and then switched to your left,' Kerrn said. 'That was not good. You must hold the sword in your right hand.'

I shook my head.

'Why? It will be easier for you this way.'

I handed her the sword and started walking

again, to catch up with the wagon. 'I hurt my shoulder and my ribs on that side,' I said.

Kerrn, walking beside me, shrugged. 'He did not hit you that hard.'

'Not Argent,' I said. 'I got hurt in Wellmet.'

She narrowed her eyes. 'You got into trouble in Wellmet, I think. What did you do?'

I didn't answer. She'd hear about it soon enough. As soon as Rowan got a letter from her mother, I guessed.

When she saw I wasn't going to tell her anything, Kerrn stalked back to the wagon, got on her horse, and rode back to the front of the line.

That night after supper, when it was time for my swordcraft lesson and Rowan held the practice sword out to me, Kerrn stepped in and took it.

Then she beat the fluff out of Argent.

Letter from former apprentice. Almost cast it in fire. Would have, but Benet awake, lucid. Asked why Conn had not visited him yet. Told him boy gone to Desh.

Benet asked —He coming back, sir?

Told him about order of exile.

Benet said nothing more.

Shadow attacks continue, worse than before. Half the factories in Twilight shut down. Sunrise locked up tight every night. Even so, people go missing. Report from acting-captain Farn, Kerrn's second, that stone corpses seen in boats on river, passing below the Night Bridge.

Went out this morning, black birds flew onto my shoulders, tugged at beard with beaks. Odd behaviour for birds. They always seemed to like the boy. Perhaps they miss him.

CHAPTER 21

At last, after a stay at a posting inn at a cross-roads and three more hot, dusty days in the desert, we reached the city. We went up and up, over a pass and round the side of a low

mountain, and there it was. Desh.

I stopped on the road to look at the city while the rest of the envoyage went on. In the middle of Desh, at the top of a rounded hill, was a gleaming white palace shaped like a star. Square pink clay-brick houses spiralled from the palace down the sides of the hill. Smudges of white and grey smoke came up from thousands of chimneys and drifted into the cloudless sky. The city was surrounded by a low, clay-brick wall, and outside of that was a wide band of burnt-dry fields.

Except on the far side of the city, where the fields ended and the land was scorched and black and pitted with wide holes and rusty machinery. What was it? Had an explosion happened there?

No. It was a mine, I realized. A slowsilver mine.

I followed the envoyage down to the city. Desh was bright with light reflecting from the pink-washed walls of the houses. The main streets were wide and lined with stalls made of faded, ragged cloth, and crowded with small, furry horses and dogs and people who stared at us and looked quickly away if we stared back. As we went along we saw empty fountains covered with cracked, coloured tiles, and tall trees with naked trunks and dried-out looking feathery leaves high above. The air smelled of spices and hot bricks. Leading off from the busy main streets were narrow, shadowed alleys. The city's magic buzzed in my ears, just the faintest sound like the hum of a gnat. The magic felt thin and faint, not like the warm, protecting magic of Wellmet.

Somehow, the envoyage got away from me. I was looking at a little lizard on a whitewashed wall, and they'd gone on along the road. I walked fast, looking around, until I caught up to them in the courtyard outside the white palace.

A servant led us inside.

We went from the brilliant-bright courtyard

through an arched doorway into a long, cool, arched hallway, then out into another courtyard, this one filled with cactuses and pink rocks and a fountain that sent water spraying up into the air and splashing into a wide, tiled pool. That might be a good place to wash in the mornings. The servant led us inside again, and up a narrow, white-washed stairway.

Then he brought us into the rooms. They had high ceilings and shuttered windows, which he threw open. The windows looked out over the city and let in the setting sun. Another one of the lizards clung with sticky toes to the wall next to the door.

'Now!' said the servant, clapping his hands. Other servants dressed in white robes appeared from the hallway. The lizard skittered away. 'You are tired from the journey! You must rest, and wash, and dress, and you will be taken to be greeted by Lord Jaggus himself!'

Rowan Forestal

We have settled into our rooms in the very glorious and luxurious palace of Lord Jaggus. Argent, Magister Nimble, and I met him the day after we arrived in Desh. The city's lord greeted us very graciously in a cool sitting room full of green plants and comfortable chairs. In one corner was a pile of pillows covered with what looked like a blanket of furs. When I looked closer I realized they were white cats with sharp pink eyes and long, snaky tails. We drank cold tea out of silver cups and ate plums and sweet cakes.

Lord Jaggus is a very smiling man, and he is young, only a year or two older than Argent. Like many people in Desh, he wears his hair in many long braids pinned up in loops on the top of his head, then wrapped up in a gauzy cloth. Though he is so young,

his hair is white, just like his odd cats. His eyes are blue and look very bright; he wears a long, flowing coat embroidered with silver and gold thread. He has a kind of contained energy. This may be a wizardly trait. Conn is the same way, as if he might burst into flames at any moment.

When I asked him about the tiny lizards that are everywhere in the city, he grimaced. _Horrid creatures_, he said. Then he looked over at his pile of cats and smiled.

I tried to ask Lord Jaggus about magical troubles, but he smilingly said that we must not discuss anything serious until we'd been properly welcomed. By that he means that he will give us a lavish ball and supper in a few days. I wonder if he is trying to delay me on purpose. Despite his oh-so-kind welcome of us, I do not trust him. He is all surface and no substance, and I don't like his cats.

I fear for Wellmet, but I must do it his way, for now.

CHAPTER 22

I stayed in Argent's rooms and read two of his books and ate plums and drank cold tea. One book was about horses, and the other was about swordcraft.

I didn't think you could learn about horses or swordcraft from reading about them. But I had nothing better to do. Reading was better than thinking about Heartsease and missing Nevery and worrying about Benet, and feeling sick-certain that an order of exile had been passed by the magisters, and wondering if the Shadows had reached Wellmet yet. I was in Desh, but what did the magic of Wellmet expect me to do here?

After a few days, Rowan and Argent were invited to a fancy ball.

While they danced to the Desh music and talked to the sorcerer-king, who smiled a lot, I leaned against a wall in a passage outside the ball-room and looked at the floor. It was covered with tiny coloured tiles that made a picture of a dragon, just like the dragon in the painting in my work-room at Heartsease.

My workroom at Heartsease before I'd destroyed it.

The dragon was made up of flame-orange tiles with paler yellow tiles on its belly and a bright red glass eye. It had a long, snaky neck and wings folded against its back. The dragon in my picture had been black, though it might've only looked black because the painting was so sooty and dirty. I remembered what Nevery had told me about dragons. *They are extinct, boy. That means you will never see a dragon.*

My stomach growled because I hadn't gotten any supper, and I was tired of plums. One of the little lizards crept along the top of the wall like a spider, then crouched in a corner. They were everywhere, the lizards. Like the black birds of Wellmet, maybe, watching things for the city's magic.

After a while Rowan came from the ball-room holding Argent's hand. Rowan laughed and gave him her slant-sly look and said something – asking him to fetch her a raspberry sherbet. He bowed and went off. She wore a dress made out of green wormsilk. Her red hair was combed down and parted on the side, and she wore a tiara made of polished grass-green adamants and diamonds wrapped in silver wire.

Rowan looked up and spotted me leaning against the wall. 'Hello, Connwaer. Why are you lurking out here in the shadows?'

'Hello, Ro,' I said. 'It's a nice tiara.'

She slanted me a glance. 'Of course it's nice. It's jewels and silver; I'm not surprised you noticed.' She stepped a little closer. 'Do you remember the ball at the Dawn Palace? When you stole your locus magicalicus from my mother's necklace?' She smiled.

I shrugged. 'Ro, I'm not going to steal your tiara.'

'I know that, Conn,' she said.

I stayed leaning against the wall. From the ballroom came the music and the smell of spices on the warm breeze.

Rowan tapped her foot on the dragon-tiled floor. 'Do you know how to dance?'

'No.'

'As part of my training in diplomacy I learned other cities' dances.' She did a few steps along with the music. 'Would you like me to teach you?'

I shook my head.

'Hmmm.' She folded her arms and looked me over. 'I believe you're homesick.'

I was. The sadness of missing Nevery and Benet and the warm kitchen at Heartsease bubbled up in me. I looked down at the floor, blinking to keep the tears from gathering in my eyes.

Rowan stepped to the middle of the hallway, standing on the dragon's tiled head, and held out her hand. 'Then I'll teach you a Wellmet dance. How would that be?'

I swallowed down my homesickness and pushed myself away from the wall. 'All right,' I said. I took Rowan's hand; it was callused from gripping a sword, and strong. 'What do I do?'

She took my other hand and put it on her waist; then she rested her other hand on my shoulder. 'This is the partner dance we do at the balls at the

Dawn Palace. The smaller partner takes the lead,' she said. 'In this case, that's you.'

'No it isn't,' I said.

She stepped out of my arms and looked at me, straight into my eyes. Then she stepped back and took my hand. 'Very well, then. First you step out with the forward foot.' She slid one of her feet forward, and I did the same thing. 'And now cross, and one-two-three.'

I tried to follow, but I wasn't very good at it, and the music was wrong.

Rowan shot me a narrow-eyed glance. '*I* lead, Connwaer.'

At that moment, Argent got back with the sherbet. 'Lady Rowan?' he asked. His voice had a good edge on it, enough to cut bread, at least.

Rowan let me go; I wiped my sweaty hands on my shirt. 'Hello, Argent,' Rowan said brightly. She gave me a friendly pat on the shoulder. 'Thank you for the dance, Conn.' She turned to face Argent and smiled at him, taking the little dish and silver spoon that he held out to her.

As they headed back into the ballroom, Argent looked back at me over his shoulder and scowled.

I stood and listened to the music for a little longer, and then went up to Argent's rooms. They were dark, so I went to the window and opened the shutters. Outside, the moon hung huge and bright overhead, making the pink buildings of the city glow in the darkness. The moonlight spilled into the room. It was bright enough to read by. I fetched a book and pushed the table up to the window and sat down.

For a while I sat there looking at the book, but not reading it. A lizard crept out onto the page and sat there without moving. The moon climbed higher. A cool breeze blew in the window. From below, I heard the sound of laughing and music from the party.

I needed to figure out what I was going to do. All I really wanted to do was go back to Wellmet to help Nevery deal with the Shadows, but the magic wouldn't let me come back until I'd done whatever it wanted me to do here. I put my head down on my folded arms to think about it.

After a while, a fluttering sound came from the window. I lifted up my head and saw a black bird, even darker than the night, land on the sill. Moonlight glinted off its wings. It cocked its head and looked at me with a keen eye. Then it looked down at the book, where the lizard was sitting.

'Hello,' I said, scrubbing my sleeve across my eyes.

The bird folded its wings and hopped inside. It looked like the same bird that had followed me in Wellmet. But what was it doing here?

'Is that you?' I asked.

It hopped closer, and I saw that it had a tube like a thick quill tied to its leg. The bird held still as I untied the tube. A paper was rolled up inside. A letter.

My hands started shaking. It was for me, and it was from Nevery.

Connwaer,
I have received your letter.

You asked after Benet. He is better, though he still suffers from headaches and his arm has not mended yet. Benet's recovery does not excuse what you have done, but it makes the magisters think somewhat less badly of you.

As you must expect, an order of exile has been passed. You are not to return to the city until this order is raised.

You cannot return here; yet you can serve Wellmet. The attacks by the Shadows continue, worse than before, and the people are frightened. We need whatever help is available. Report on what you have discovered about the Shadows, about the state of the city of Desh and its magic, about how Lady Rowan's negotiations with the sorcerer-king go on, about Jaggus's use of magic. If you have received this letter, it means my attempt with the bird has been successful. I expect to receive from you at least one letter every five days, sent by the bird.

— Nevery

I flattened out the paper against the tabletop and read it again. The moonlight made the letters look black-dark against the white paper. Benet was better, he said. A big part of the dark emptiness inside of me went away.

Report on what you have discovered, Nevery said. But I hadn't discovered anything. I'd been so busy feeling sad that I hadn't been paying attention. How could I have been so stupid?

CHAPTER 23

I decided to start discovering things for Nevery right away. If I'd had a locus magicalicus I would've done the embero spell and turned myself into a cat, because as a cat I made a very good spy. Instead, as the night had gotten cooler, I pulled on my black sweater and took off my boots. Leaving the bird perched on the windowsill with the lizard, I eased out into the dark hallway and down the stairs.

I was in luck. The fancy ball was breaking up. At the ballroom, the sorcerer-king stood in a wide doorway talking in a low voice to another man. Three guards waited for Jaggus, standing stiff as pokers in long-skirted white coats with red trim and white trousers with red boots. And swords. They stayed behind Jaggus, which meant I had a good view of him from the hallway where I crouched in a patch of shadow.

The sorcerer-king didn't wear his locus magicalicus on a chain or a necklace outside his clothes. He had one hand thrust down into a pocket of his long-skirted white coat. Maybe the stone was in there. If I could get past the guards it wouldn't be hard to pick his pocket to have a look at his locus magicalicus.

In the doorway, Jaggus glanced toward me and

I turned to stone until he looked away again. He hadn't seen me.

He finished talking to the other man and I eased back behind a giant clay pot as he passed down the hallway, followed by his three guards. I cat-footed after them, keeping to the shadows. They wound around deeper into the palace until they came to a door painted red with a brass handle and lock.

Jaggus opened the door with a key he pulled from his pocket. A triple-flick count-two lock, from the sound of it. That was odd.

To Nevery,

I am very glad Benet is better. Please tell him that I am sorry.

You said I should discover everything I can and report it to you, one letter every five days, so that's what I'll do. It's a long, long way to Wellmet. I wonder how the bird flies there and back here so quickly. Maybe it's got a piece of the magic in it.

Something is strange about the sorcerer-king. Maybe he sent the Shadows to Wellmet, but I can't tell for certain if he did or not. The strange thing is that he has his rooms locked up with a key and a lock.

Nevery, wouldn't a wizard use a spell to lock up his rooms, especially a workroom? Just like you use a spell to lock your grimoire and the magisters use spells to lock the gates to the islands?

He doesn't wear his locus magicalicus on a chain the way Pettivox did. I wonder if he doesn't carry it on him at all. I'll try to find out. Even though his rooms are locked with a puzzle lock, I can get in if I know when he's going to be away.

That's all I could discover so far, but I'll keep looking around as much as I can, and then I'll write and tell you.

From,

Connwaer

Rowan Forestal

Dealing with the sorcerer-king is frustrating. He is hospitable and friendly, but he will not give a clear answer to any of my questions. Magister Nimble reports that Lord Jaggus answered every one of his questions about the magic of Desh, which means Nimble is satisfied that our host is not responsible for sending the Shadows to Wellmet.

I am becoming more certain that Nimble is a fool.

I can't be certain of anything until I have proof. The question is, how to get it?

A packet of letters from Mother arrived today. She asks how our meetings with Lord Jaggus go on, and describes further Shadow attacks in the Sunrise. She also wrote that she and the magisters have issued an order of exile against Conn, which means he cannot

return to Wellmet until it is lifted. I'd suspected something had happened to force him to leave, but I didn't realize it was this bad: Heartsease destroyed, Nevery's manservant severely injured, the magisters in an uproar. Mother advises me that I shouldn't have permitted Conn to join the envoyage, and that now that we have reached Desh, I should order him to leave.

I absolutely refuse to obey her. Heartsease was half destroyed already. Conn was just finishing what Magister Nevery started twenty years ago. Has nobody thought of that? And while the damage done is appalling, it makes perfectly clear what Conn has been saying all along, that he can somehow do magic with pyrotechnics, which means he may be right about the magic itself. I half believe they have exiled him simply because his ideas are dangerous and they are afraid.

No wonder he has been so quiet. He is quiet any-

way, but since he joined the envoyage he's hardly said a word. I thought he was being sullen, and I should have seen that it was because he is desperately unhappy. I feel like a poor sort of friend for not realizing this before.

I have tried to find him, but he's disappeared, though Argent says he comes back in late at night to sleep before slipping away again. Next I will ask Kerrn, because I suspect that as guard captain she has been keeping a close eye on Conn.

CHAPTER 24

The next night, after the usual dinner party had ended and the palace had quieted down into the night, I sat on the floor in the hallway outside Jaggus's rooms in the shadow of a giant clay pot, trying not to fall asleep. He'd gone in hours before. An oil lantern burned low beside his door.

Down at the other end of the dark hallway, a bit of shadow broke off from the rest of the shadows and hopped over the tile floor, coming toward me.

I sat up and blinked, and saw that it was a black bird. It had a quill strapped to its leg, and the quill went *tick tick* against the floor every time the bird took a hop.

Keeping an eye on Jaggus's door, I went to meet the bird and carried it over to my hiding place. It let me take the quill off its leg. A letter from Nevery.

Connwaer,

I know you well enough, boy, to understand your cryptic references. In your letter you wrote that you will 'try to find out' if Jaggus carries his locus magicalicus on him. And 'I can get in' to his workroom. You mean you're going to pick his pocket, boy, and pick the lock of his workroom. This is far too dangerous. If you were caught, Lady Rowan would have no reason to protect you, as she knows by now that you have been exiled, and I could do nothing from here. Also, you know well enough the effect of evil magics on a locus magicalicus. You remember prying into my family collection of locus stones and touching my great-aunt Alwae's stone. It made you sick, did it not? If Jaggus is responsible for creating the Shadows, his stone

will be even more corrupt than Alwae's.
   Be careful, boy, and don't be stupid.
   The situation in Wellmet grows worse every
day. I rely on your information.
— Nevery

It wasn't very good advice. I couldn't learn anything just by watching. Still, I watched Jaggus's workroom door for the rest of the night. Sitting against the wall in the dark quiet, I thought about Nevery's letter. He'd called me *boy*. Maybe he wasn't quite so angry with me anymore. And he sounded worried. He didn't need to worry; I wouldn't get caught picking a pocket or a lock. And what did he mean by *the situation in Wellmet*? The Shadows, clear as clear, but what were they doing?

Just before dawn, Jaggus came out of his workroom. He stepped out the door and looked both ways down the hall, but he didn't see me in my hiding place. Then he turned to snick-close the lock and paced softly away. I started to follow him, when I noticed something.

On the floor by the workroom door. Something glowed a little against the tiles. I went down on my knees and peered at it.

Just the heel of his footprint, outlined in

something purple-black and glowing. After a moment, it disappeared with a sizzle of acrid smoke.

Darksilver.

The next night, during the dinner party, I decided to have a look in Jaggus's rooms while he was away, just to see what he had in there.

After he'd gone out, I snick-picked the lock and crept in, locking the door behind me. Oil lanterns had been left burning but turned low, so the rooms were full of shadows and bits of light glinting off all the gold draperies and glass tiles. But I wasn't interested in finery.

I slunk through the rooms, finding nothing, until I came to a library.

Here was Jaggus's treasure. I found a lantern and prowled through the shelves of books and scrolls and stitch-bound treatises. He had books full of the swirly, Desh writing. He had a copy of *both* of Jaspers's writings on pyrotechnics, written in the same runes we used in Wellmet.

I could read fast. It would only take a little while, and he'd be gone until dawn. I grabbed the treatise off the shelf and found a lexicon, and sat down with the lantern at the long table that ran down the middle of the room between the rows of shelves.

A long time later I looked up because I heard the rustle of cloth and the soft scuff of a slipper on the carpet. Someone had come up behind me and stood looking over my shoulder.

'Ah, I must have left my door unlocked!' he said.

Jaggus, I realized. Drats. Why hadn't I heard him come into the library? He must have a secret way in. The back of my neck shivered. He knew very well that he hadn't left the door unlocked.

'What do you read?' he asked. He spoke with an accent, almost like his tongue was a knife and it sharpened the words so they sounded pointed and prickling.

I turned the book and held it up to show him the title stamped in gold on the front cover.

'Ah!' The sorcerer-king moved to the side, where he could see me better, and where I could see him. Even though he had to know that I'd picked the lock to get in, he was smiling. Pretending to be my friend. 'You have an interest in pyrotechnics?'

'Yes,' I said.

He leaned over and tapped the book. His fingernails were painted gold. 'This is the second treatise of Jaspers. My own rare copy. Have you read the first treatise?'

I nodded.

'And I assume you have read the Prattshaw book.'

I nodded again.

'Hmmm! Who are you, precisely?'

'I'm Connwaer,' I said. No point in lying about it.

'Ah!' He rested his finger on his lips, then

pointed at me. 'A true name, one that is meaning-ful to the magic. It means *black bird*, I believe.'

Is meaningful to the magic, he said. Did he know the magic was a living being, just like I did, and that spellwords were its language?

'Here in Desh, Connwaer also means *black shadow*,' he said.

I blinked.

'Many words, as we use them, have two mean-ings, so that we mean two different things when we say them.' He smiled, and when he did, I real-ized that even though his hair was white, he wasn't much older than I was. 'You do remind me of a black shadow,' he said.

I looked down at myself. I was wearing the black sweater Benet had given me, and my hair had gotten shaggy again and hung down in my eyes. But I had a feeling he meant that I looked dark, like a shadow, *and* that he'd seen me watch-ing him.

'I am the lord of this city, Jaggus,' he said,

settling into a chair. 'Also a true name.'

I wondered what *Jaggus* meant; I glanced toward the end of the table, where I'd left the lexicon.

'Now, my shadow, you have not yet answered my question.'

I thought back over our conversation. *Who are you?* he'd asked. Oh. 'I'm from Wellmet.'

'Yes. A servant of the Lady Rowan's companion, Sir Argent?'

I took a deep breath. 'Yes,' I answered, hating the taste of the lie in my mouth.

'Pyrotechnics seem an odd interest for a servant.'

I shrugged. Drats. I needed to not talk to him anymore. He was too sharp.

'And from Wellmet. I know a man from Wellmet who has an interest in pyrotechnics. Perhaps you know him, too? His name is Flinglas.'

Nevery, he meant.

'Do you know him?' Jaggus asked.

I nodded.

'He is a friend, then?'

I looked down at the book, at the gold letters stamped on the cover. 'No.'

'Ah. Not a friend. But not an enemy, either, I think. He is, perhaps, your master?'

I shook my head.

'I see.' Jaggus got to his feet. He blinked, and in his eyes the black pupils widened like a window opening up on the blackest night sky, no stars. He stared at me for another moment, then, on silent feet, he crossed the carpeted floor and went out the door.

I see, he'd said. I wondered what he saw with his strange eyes. I had a feeling he already knew who I was and what I was up to.

I got up and went to the end of the table, to the lexicon. *Jaggus*. It meant *destroy*. But its second meaning, in small type, was *broken*.

I wasn't sure what to think of that.

CHAPTER 25

After leaving Jaggus's rooms in the grey light of morning, I crept up the stairs toward Argent's rooms. Rowan was lying in wait for me.

She sat hunched on a step, wrapped in a robe over her nightgown, with a lantern next to her.

'Hello, Ro,' I whispered.

She looked crossly up at me and rubbed her eyes. 'What are you up to, Connwaer?'

I sat on the step next to her. 'I have to find out what Jaggus is doing.'

'I believe that is my job,' she said.

'Are *you* getting anywhere?' I asked.

She rested her chin on her knees and stared down the dark well of the stairs. 'I can't tell,' she said at last. 'Though I agree with you that he's up to something. I must try talking further with him.'

But talking was taking too long.

We sat quietly. I leaned my shoulder against hers. The light from the lantern flickered golden against the whitewashed walls.

'He's not going to tell you anything,' I said at last. 'Tomorrow night I'll have a look in his workroom.' He had a secret door in that library somewhere, and I could find it and get in.

At that, Rowan sat up and glared at me. Her hair hung in tangles around her face. 'No!' she said.

Her voice echoed off the walls. The door to

the right of the top of the stairs creaked open, and Argent peered out. He came down a few steps, blinking, in bare feet and a spotted blue nightgown. 'What is the matter, Lady Rowan?' he asked.

She didn't even glance at him. 'What if you're caught, Conn? Have you thought of that?'

I shrugged.

She gritted her teeth and made a noise that sounded like *grrrr*. 'I could order you, as a member of the envoyage, not to do it.'

'I'm not a member of your envoyage,' I said.

'Do as you're told, boy,' Argent said.

I glanced over my shoulder at him. 'I'm not your servant, Argent,' I said.

Rowan stood up and glared down at me, her hands clenched. In the lantern light, her eyes gleamed silver and furious. 'So you'll just do as you please, Conn, is that what you're saying?'

I stood up to face her. 'Ro, things in Wellmet are getting worse. We have to do *some-thing*.'

She closed her eyes and took a deep breath. 'Argent,' she said. 'Please allow Conn and me to continue this conversation in private.'

'Of course, Lady Rowan,' he said. He bowed and went back into his rooms.

Rowan opened her eyes. 'Yes,' she said. 'You're right. My mother's letters have not been specific, but I suspect things in Wellmet have gotten very bad. We have to get on with it.'

Good. 'Then I'll sneak into Jaggus's workroom to see what he's up to.'

'No, you won't,' Rowan said. 'I need to try one more time to talk to him, to see if I can figure out why he's sending the Shadows against us. If it is him.'

'It's him,' I said. The darksilver footprint proved that.

'Maybe.' She shook her head slowly. 'I need one last chance to try diplomacy.'

I didn't say anything. I wasn't sure, exactly, what *diplomacy* was.

'All right?' Rowan said.

All right, if she really wanted me to wait. I nodded.

Rowan Forestal

I have insisted that Lord Jaggus give me a tour of one of the slowsilver mines, and to my surprise he agreed. Oddly, he suggested that I bring Argent and also Argent's servant. By that he means Conn, which means Conn isn't as good a spy as he thinks he is.

    I thought carefully about my request. Slowsilver is associated with magic. And Desh is the supplier of much of the Peninsular Duchies' slowsilver. Yet that supply, according to the pyrotechnist Sparks, has dwindled. I suspect that something is wrong with the slowsilver mines, something that will explain the nature of Wellmet's danger.

TREE & LEAF

Dear Nevery,

You were right about lockpicking Jaggus's door. He caught me at it. I didn't realize that you knew him. He talks like he knows you, anyway.

I haven't gotten a look at Jaggus's locus magicalicus yet, and yes, I'll be careful when I try for his pocket, and when I check his workroom. The only proof I have so far of anything is a darksilver footprint. He's up to something, sure as sure, but I don't know what, and I don't know what Wellmet has to do with it. I will find out.

The magic was right to send me here, though. Hello to Benet.

— Conn

ᚨ○◇⌶ ᚨ○ ୪○୪ ⌶○◌◡◡

○◌◌ ∧○○◌◌ ◌⌶◌◡◌

∧○◡◌ ∧○◡◌◌

—◌

I was at the table in the room I shared with Argent, finishing up a letter to Nevery. One of the city's lizards, the same one, I suspected, peered into the inkpot and then, making footprints along the edge of the paper, came to sit next to my hand.

Across the room, Argent lay on his bed eating plums and reading his book about swordcraft. He had his boots off, and his feet smelled like mouldy cheese.

'Go fetch me a pot of tea, boy,' Argent said, and took a juicy bite of plum.

I ignored him. When the ink on my letter was dry, I tipped the lizard onto the table and folded the paper. A bird would be along soon, I expected.

Knock-knock-knock at the door.

'Go and see who it is,' Argent said.

I folded the paper again and rolled it into a tight tube so it would fit into the bird's quill.

KNOCK KNOCK KNOCK!

'Go see who's at the door!' Argent said loudly, and when I didn't he picked up his boot and threw it at me. I ducked, and it flew past me and out the window.

Rowan flung the door open. 'Neither of you

could be bothered, I suppose,' she said. She glared at me. 'What are you laughing at, Connwaer?'

'Stupid fool,' Argent grumbled.

'You'd better go get it,' I said to him.

'I'll send a *servant* for it,' Argent said.

Not me, then.

'Diplomacy,' Rowan muttered. 'Patience.' She shook her head. 'I was going to ask if you two wanted to join me on a tour of a slowsilver mine.'

I stood up so fast that my chair crashed to the floor. Yes, I wanted to join her.

'Does he have to come?' Argent asked, getting to his feet.

'Lord Jaggus invited him,' Rowan said, giving me a raised-eyebrows look. 'I'll meet you outside.' She left the room, slamming the door behind her.

So the sorcerer-king wanted me along. Sure as sure he knew what I was up to. Maybe he wanted to keep an eye on me. Still, I wasn't going to miss seeing a slowsilver mine.

As I cleaned my pen and capped the bottle of ink, the lizard crept to the edge of the table and looked up at me with its sharp black eyes. 'D'you want to come, too?' I asked. As an answer, it leaped off the table, landing on my sleeve, clinging with its sticky toes. I picked it off and dropped it into my coat pocket. Safer in there.

To get into the mine we climbed into a big bucket on a chain that lowered us down into a dark shaft like a well but without the sparkle of water at the bottom.

The air was hot and sooty. *Creak-rattle-creak* and we went lower and lower and the dark grew thicker. We stayed quiet, me and Rowan and Argent, two white-coated guards, Jaggus, and the minekeeper, a fat man with a beard and jingling bracelets on his wrists.

'So!' said the minekeeper. His voice echoed in the darkness. 'We go down a bit farther and a short way farther into the mine and we will show you the slowsilver extraction facility.'

Creak-rattle and down we went for a long way, until we stopped with a jerk. I could feel the others close by in the bucket, and hear the rustle of their clothes and their breathing, but the dark pressed up against my face like a dusty pillow.

'Ah,' muttered the minekeeper. 'Here we are.' I heard stone striking stone, saw a spark, and then a candle flared. The keeper unchained the gate and we got out of the bucket. The candle flame pushed back the heavy darkness, and we stood blinking in a faint circle of light.

'Why don't you use werelights?' I asked, and – *ights, ights, ights* came back as an echo.

They all stared at me. Jaggus's eyes grew wide and dark, then turned blue again.

'Oh, no,' the minekeeper said. The bracelets jingled on his wrists. 'Werelights are unsafe in the mine. Use of magic is strictly forbidden here. The magic, ah' – he glanced aside at Jaggus and paused – 'it ah, makes the mine very, very unsafe.

I have an oil lantern just here, and it will give us more light.' Taking the candle with him, he went to fetch a lantern.

As good a chance as any. In the darkness, Jaggus was just a shadow, his two guards looming up behind him. I edged closer and – *quick hands* – dipped into the pocket of his long-skirted coat. Empty. Drats. I reached around him and tried the other pocket. Nothing. He didn't have his locus magicalicus on him.

The keeper came back with a lantern. By its light I could see that we were in a tunnel with soot-blackened walls and a rock ceiling that slanted down over our heads.

'This way, if you please,' said the keeper.

We went through the tunnel, the keeper, Rowan and Jaggus, then the two guards, then me and Argent.

Up ahead, the lantern light flickered against the walls. A faint *thump, thump, thump* came up through the ground, making my legs tremble. In the distance I heard the echoey sound of metal grinding on metal. It reminded me of the workroom under Dusk House – and of the device Crowe and Pettivox had made to imprison the magic. It wasn't the same thing, but something about the mine wasn't right. In my pocket, the lizard was trembling. And the high-pitched buzzing sound of Desh's magic was gone. I'd gotten used to the buzz, just as I was used to the warm presence of Wellmet's magic. But the minekeeper was right – the magic did not belong in the mine. Something was wrong here, but I didn't know what.

Beside me, Argent paced along with his hands shoved into his pockets and his head down.

'You all right?' I asked.

He flicked a look up at the ceiling and hunched his shoulders. 'Be quiet, *boy*.'

I shrugged.

'Just a bit farther,' the keeper called from ahead, and – *arther, arther, arther* came the echo.

'What is slowsilver for, anyway?' Argent muttered.

For magic, I was about to say, when we came out of the tunnel and into the mine itself.

Lanterns were hung up on wires along the walls, which arched up to a dark ceiling way above. To our right, built into the stone walls, was a huge rusty-metal device, all gears and pistons and steam; it groaned as a giant metal wheel turned round, then stopped. Water gushed from a pipe taller than I was; then the flow slowed to a trickle-drip. So this is where all the city's water was – running the mine's machinery. A few workers stood around the machine, their faces black with soot. They watched us; they'd shut down the machine while we were there, and would start up again when we left.

Before us was a black pit so wide I could see the lanterns on the other side of it as tiny points of light like stars. A narrow path went around the edge of the pit, spiralling down into the darkness.

Workers carrying packs loaded with stone plodded up the path; more workers with empty packs headed down.

The minekeeper pointed at the pit. 'This was once filled with slowsilver,' he said. 'Imagine it if you will, like a silver lake here under the ground, with streams of slowsilver flowing through the cracks in the rock. So beautiful.' He kept talking, telling about other mines and other lakes beneath the city, and underground rivers of slowsilver.

The lizard poked its head out of my pocket; I lifted it out and put it on my shoulder so it could see. I could imagine the lake the keeper was talking about. But it was gone, leaving behind an empty, echoing hole. The rivers of slowsilver had all run dry.

What is slowsilver for, Argent had asked. I remembered a line from the Prattshaw book: *Slowsilver is a contrafusive which is purposed for attracting and constraining or, that is to say, confining the magic.*

Pettivox had used slowsilver in the prisoning device to keep the magic in.

To keep the magic in. Slowsilver attracted magic. Was the magical being of Desh tied to this place because of its slowsilver? And if the slowsilver was being stripped away by mining – wouldn't the being's connection to the city weaken? I shook my head. It didn't make sense. Why would Jaggus, a wizard, want to weaken the magic of his own city? Surely he'd want it to be stronger, because that would make him stronger.

Jaggus stepped up beside me. 'It is an amazing operation, I think. What do you think of it, my shadow?' he asked.

'I don't understand it,' I said. 'Why are you doing this?'

He smiled and stroked one of his long white braids. 'It is a mystery, is it not?' His eyes shifted and he saw the lizard on my shoulder. 'Horrid creatures,' he said. 'Little spies, always watching.'

With quick hands he snatched the lizard off my shoulder, dropping it onto the stone floor. Before it could skitter away, before I could stop him, he lowered his foot and slowly pressed down. I heard the *crack* of tiny bones.

No! I stared at him.

He gazed back at me, his eyes gone wide and dark like the pit. He ground his foot harder against the rock floor. In my head, the buzz of the Desh magic gave a high shriek, then quieted. Then he scraped off the bottom of his shoe and walked away to where Rowan and Argent stood with the minekeeper.

I stared down at the smear on the rock floor that had been the little lizard. A shivery chill crept down my neck. He'd killed one of his own city's lizards. That would be like me or Nevery killing one of the black birds of Wellmet. We wouldn't, not ever. The air in the cavern grew thicker. I stepped to the edge of the pit and stared down. Was there just the smallest sparkle of slowsilver down there in the darkness? I leaned forward to see better. No, it was just dark.

I straightened and stepped away from the edge of the pit. Jaggus was killing Desh, his own city, the same as he killed the lizard. I didn't know why. But I would find out. And I would stop him if I could.

CHAPTER 27

I'd have just one chance.

After we got back from the mine, Jaggus went to dinner with Rowan and Argent, which meant I had time to sneak into his rooms and find his hidden work-room. Maybe his locus magicalicus would be there. Maybe I'd find a clue about why he was

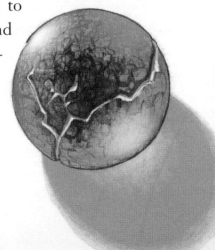

killing his own city with the slowsilver mining — and sending his Shadows after *my* city.

Keeping an ear out for guards, I picked the lock to his rooms and eased the door open, then closed it behind me and relocked it. Through the rooms to the library, where Jaggus had snuck up on me.

The secret door was easy to find, once I knew to look for it. Behind a tasselled, gold curtain was a low door. It wasn't even locked. I turned the knob, ducked my head, and, bringing my lantern with me, went in.

Jaggus's workroom was long, narrow, and high-ceilinged. I couldn't see down to the back wall of the room; it was too dark. Dust was scattered across the stone floor. I looked for Shadows but didn't see any.

On a table were four wide glass bowls, each with a curving lip around its inside edge. In three of the bowls was slowsilver, swirling like melted mirrors. Pieces like snails broke off from the shiny surface and crept up the sides of the bowls like they were trying to escape, but they couldn't get past the lip and flowed back down again.

In the fourth bowl was something else. The glass had darkened, as if it'd been smoked. I leaned over the table to peer in. In the middle of the bowl was Jaggus's locus magicalicus.

It was a jewel stone, like mine had been, but round and polished, and the deep red of old blood. It sat in the middle of the bowl in a puddle of sizzling purple-black darksilver. In a ring around it was slowsilver, pulling away as if repelled by the stone, and straining toward the edge of the bowl. As I watched, a slowsilver snail was sucked away from the ring and pulled in toward the locus magicalicus. When it touched the surface of the stone, it shimmered and tried to writhe away, and then darkened to tarnished black. After a moment, it oozed into the sizzling puddle and started to glow purple-black.

He was making darksilver.

At the edge of my vision, I caught a glimpse of something, and I looked quickly up. At the other end of the room, Shadows rose up out of the darkness and hovered there, watching me. Clouds of dust seethed around them. I stared back at them and held my breath. Their purple-black eyes pulsed. But they stayed back, like they were behind a glass wall. No orders, I guessed. Or maybe afraid of the locus magicalicus.

So he was making Shadows, too.

This was proof, then. He was using magic to come after Wellmet, maybe after he finished off Desh. No more diplomacy. I had to do something, and do it *now*.

Trying to ignore the Shadows, I peered more closely at Jaggus's locus stone. Its surface was smooth, but at its centre was a black, rotted heart.

Without a locus stone, Jaggus couldn't make any more Shadows to send to Wellmet.

Taking a deep breath, I reached down into the bowl and snatched the locus stone out of the puddle of darksilver.

A wave of sickness flowed out from the stone and up my arm. I dropped the stone, and went down on my knees, dizzy and retching. Black spots swam before my eyes.

Good thing I hadn't had any dinner. I wiped my mouth and looked round for the stone. It had rolled into the middle of the floor.

I got shakily to my feet. This was a powerful stone, and I knew I couldn't destroy it now.

I'd have to steal it. I searched the room until I found a drawstring leather pouch full of shredded leaves. After emptying out the leaves, I brought the pouch close to the locus stone where it lay on the floor and opened its mouth wide.

Taking a deep breath, I picked up the locus stone and dropped it into the bag. Then I had another round of coughing up my stomach.

After the dark spots had cleared away and my

stomach decided to go back to its usual place, I got to my feet.

I had to get out of there quick, before Jaggus came in. And then away from Desh as fast as I could.

Rowan –

I know you didn't want me to do it, but I stole Jaggus's locus magicalicus, and I'm leaving Desh tonight. I had to, Ro. The magic of Desh is very thin and faint. I think Jaggus plans to use his locus stone to destroy Desh, and Wellmet will be next, sure as sure. He was using his locus stone to make darksilver for the Shadows, I saw them in his workroom.

I am going south, away from Wellmet. You need to leave Desh as soon as you can. Go back to Wellmet and warn them about Jaggus.

– Conn

CHAPTER 28

In the darkest part of the night, I set off into the desert wearing a sand-coloured robe over my shirt and trousers, a head scarf wrapped over my face, my knife in my pocket and Kerrn's knife in my boot, a couple of copper locks on a fraying purse string that I nicked from Argent, and a canteen slung over my shoulder. I didn't have time to steal any food.

I put the leather pouch with Jaggus's locus magicalicus in it into my pocket.

I didn't head down the road toward Wellmet, figuring that would be the first direction Jaggus would search. Instead, I went through the dried, brown fields and then onto a rutted caravan track leading away from the city, toward the south.

Desh fell away behind me, its lights getting fainter as the sky above me turned grey. Before long, the sun leaped up into the sky.

The sorcerer-king would send trackers after me, sure as sure. They would come this way eventually. But I couldn't go off the road or the thorns would cut me to pieces. I walked fast. And I tried not to think of what Nevery would do if he could see me now. I hadn't gotten a chance to send my last letter. He'd be furious when it didn't arrive on time. *More trouble than you're worth,* he'd say. And Rowan. She would be even more furious, and she'd be right to be angry. But I hadn't had much of a choice.

At midday, I stopped to rest in the shade of a

tall cactus and drank half of my water. As I sat there, a black bird swooped down and landed on the ground next to me.

'Hello,' I said.

It didn't have a quill strapped to its leg.

'Thirsty?' I asked.

It hopped up to perch on my bent knees, gripping the cloth of my robe with its claws, and drank water from my cupped hand, dipping its beak in and tipping its head back. It hadn't brought a letter, but it was a Wellmet bird, sure as sure. Maybe it was the magic's way of saying that I'd done the right thing, stealing Jaggus's locus stone.

I went on with the bird on my shoulder.

After a few hours of head-down trudging, I came to a tiny village made of mud and palm leaves and set on a crossroads. The sun was setting, a gold coin hanging over the distant mountains, and long shadows lay across the village square. I walked across the dry, packed ground to the public well, a covered hole in the ground with a leather bucket on a rope sitting next to it. The black bird fluttered off my shoulder to the ground beside the bucket. I shoved the cover aside and dropped the bucket down, then pulled it up and scooped up a palm full of water, then another.

Something bumped against my fingers – smooth, cool skin. I tilted the bucket to get a better look at whatever it was.

'Two coppers to drink, young sir,' said a creaky voice.

I looked up. An old person wrapped in brown rags stood beside the well. She – I reckoned it was a she – poked a wrinkled old claw of a hand out of her tattered robe.

I nodded at the bucket. 'Is that a frog in there?'

She cackled. 'This is Frogtown. Frogs in the water is good luck. Two coppers to drink.'

I dug my purse string out of the pocket of my robe. I had four copper locks; well, I had nothing else to spend them on. 'If I give you four, will it buy some food?' I pointed at the bucket. 'I'm so hungry, I could eat that frog.' In a pot pie with gravy and carrots and peas, like Benet made.

The water-crone cackled again. 'Hah!' She cocked

her head, and I saw a beady blue eye peeking out of the shawls covering her head. 'Somebody after you?'

Sure as sure, somebody was after me. My feet were getting itchy, needing to go on.

'Trackers?' she asked.

I shrugged.

'Hah.' She whirled and scuttled away, across the dusty square, to one of the mud houses. I crouched by the well and drank more water, and filled my canteen. I held out more water to the bird, and it drank.

After a short while, she came back. 'Here.' She handed me a little package made of palm leaves; peeking inside, I saw flat bread and goat cheese and a few plump green olives threaded on a string.

I nodded thanks and handed her the coins.

'Four more,' she said, stowing the money in her ragged robe, 'and I'll tell the trackers I didn't see you.'

'That's all I've got.' I stood up, looking toward the horizon. The sun had gone down behind the mountains and the shadows were turning purple. Time to get going.

'Full moon tonight,' the water-crone said.

'Good travelling.'

'Thanks,' I said. The bird flapped up to perch on my shoulder.

The old woman turned away. 'Frogs in the bucket is good luck,' she said over her shoulder.

I hoped they were. I put the packet of food in the pocket of my robe with my knife and my empty purse string, and headed out of the village, into the growing darkness.

I walked all night, until morning came, soft and rosy. By midday, I got to a place where the road narrowed and pressed up against an overhang of the soft, orange stone. On the other side of the road, a bare rock face sloped downward to a cliff, which in turn dropped away to a ravine far below. If I slipped off the road here, I'd slide straight to the edge and then fall to the bottom of that cliff. As I walked, one hand on the rock wall to guide me, pebbles slid beneath my feet and fell tumbling down the slope. I shook the tiredness out of my head and went on.

At last, as the sun was setting in a bonfire over the distant mountains, I followed the caravan road out of the orange rocks and back onto the desert floor. I went on, limping, as the sky grew darker. The flat bread and olives were long gone, and I was hollow with hunger. I missed Nevery and Wellmet. I imagined that each step took me closer to home, that I was walking through the dark tunnels to Heartsease, that I would come up the stairs and across the courtyard and into the kitchen, where Benet would have biscuits and bacon waiting for me.

Then I fell.

My hands were in my pockets, so I fell straight onto the road, bumping my chin. Ow. The bird tumbled to the ground with a squawk. I closed my eyes and rested my face against the cooling sand and pebbles. It felt like the most comfortable bed.

Behind me, a perfect travelling moon rose over the desert. The trackers were coming. The bird pecked at my shoulder and at my face. But I didn't care. I didn't even bother moving off the road. I just closed my eyes and went to sleep.

Rowan Forestal

Curse Connwaer to the very ends of the world. Kerrn was not surprised. *He is a thief*, she said. *Stealing is what he does.*

That is true. But Conn has proof of Jaggus's danger to Wellmet, and he is right that we must return at once so we can plan how to act against the sorcerer-king.

Meanwhile, I can't let Conn die in the desert, or be captured by Jaggus's men.

I took Captain Kerrn aside and asked her to track Conn down and bring him, and the jewel he stole, quietly to the posting inn on the way to Wellmet. I'll meet them there with the rest of the envoyage.

Whatever happens, I told her, *don't let Conn fall into Jaggus's hands.*

Kerrn set off at once.

⊟⊙   ⊼⊗⌐⊟   ⊼⋀ᘛ⊙   ⌂⋔

⊥⊙⏝⊙⊓⋀⊙   ⌐⌂⌐⊟⊙꞉

CHAPTER 29

I woke up with the rising sun in my face and the heat pressing down on me like a heavy hand. My mouth felt like Nevery's study: dusty and full of paper. The bird was gone. I wondered where. I sat up, creaking in every bone, and looked back toward the orange rocks, far in the distance.

I saw a dark spot there, wavery

from the heat rising from the ground. I shaded my eyes with my hand and squinted. The dark spot jiggled up and down on the road.

A man. Riding a horse. Tracker.

Drats.

I jumped to my feet and, the fear jolting through my legs, ran a few steps.

I stopped. I was being stupid. The tracker was riding a horse. I wasn't going to outrun him. Catching my breath, I gulped more water from my canteen, then paced along the road, looking for a likely spot.

There – an opening in the thorny scrub. Going back along the road where I'd walked, trying not to look at the black spot, I found a branch with a few dried leaves on it and, walking backward, used it to wipe out my trail until I came to the opening. I backed into it, still brushing out my footprints, and went along a short way.

Then I doubled back again, threw the branch away, and crouched in the bushes, hidden.

At first, the desert around me was silent, then I started hearing scratchings like little clawed feet scurrying over sand and rock, and faint slitherings, and the chirping of birds. The air smelled of hot sand – and of my own sweaty smell; I hoped the tracker didn't have a good nose or my plan wouldn't work.

At last, I heard the *shuff shuff* of horse hooves on the sandy road, not far away. They went past, but I didn't move. If the tracker was any good, he was not going to be fooled by the brushed-out footprints.

Sure enough, after a few minutes, the sound of hooves came back. Then the creak of leather and two human feet crunching onto the ground. The tracker ventured onto the side trail.

Slowly, I lowered my head onto my knees, closed my eyes, and then kept as still as a mouse under the eye of a hawk. The desert fell silent. The tracker's footsteps went stealthily past the bushes where I was hiding. I waited ten breaths, and then

I slithered out of my hiding place and raced down the trail, toward the road.

Behind me, I heard the tracker shout, but he wasn't going to catch me. I burst out onto the road — there was the tracker's horse, all saddled and ready to go, its reins wrapped around a thorny branch.

Perched on its saddle was the bird.

It had led the tracker right to me, the traitor.

Pushing it out of the way, I grabbed at the reins and put a foot in the stirrup. The horse shied sideways and the bird flew up with a squawk. With a shout, the tracker raced out onto the trail, lowered his head, and bulled into me with his shoulder. We both went sprawling onto the ground. I rolled away and gave him a kick in the ribs, then scrambled up and went for the horse again.

I clutched its mane to pull myself up, and it shook its head; the tracker grabbed me from behind and threw me to the ground, then leaped on me. I went for my knife; I was just wrestling it out of my pocket when the tracker knocked it from my hand

and held his own knife to my throat.

'I will use it,' he growled. 'Keep still.'

No, he wasn't going to catch me that easily. I wriggled and groped after the other knife in my boot. The tracker ripped off my head scarf and held his knife under my chin. The blade's sharp edge drew a line of blood on the skin of my neck.

I kept still.

The tracker loomed over me, knee on my chest, breathing hard. In the struggle, the head scarf had come off, and a blond braid like a rope hung down. Not a tracker, I realized. A friend. I felt a sudden flare of hope. 'Kerrn!' I gasped.

She didn't answer, and her ice-chip blue eyes stayed cold. She took her knee off my chest and hauled me to my feet and over to the horse, which had its reins still tangled in the bush. She reached into a saddlebag and pulled out several lengths of thin rope. Not speaking, she took my hands, looped a piece of rope around them, and tied it off.

I stared at her. 'What're you doing?'

Her eyes narrowed. 'Stay quiet.' Using another, longer length of rope, she tethered my tied hands to a loop of leather on her saddle. Then she turned back to me. 'Show me what you stole, thief.'

Oh, no.

Kerrn had always thought of me as a thief, not a wizard, and I *had* stolen the jewel, that was true enough. But I couldn't let her touch Jaggus's locus magicalicus. It would kill her, sure as sure. I shook my head and stepped back, but the tether rope brought me up short.

Kerrn lunged toward me, grabbed me by the front of my robe, and backed me against the horse, which stood calmly still. I tried to squirm away while she searched me, first one pocket, tossing the empty purse string on the ground, then the other, where she found the leather bag. Letting me go, she started to open it.

'No!' I shouted, and with my bound hands knocked the leather bag from her hands. It flew through the air and landed with a soft *thunk* on the sand.

In one stride, she reached the bag and bent to pick it up.

'No – don't touch it!' I strained toward her, held back by the tether.

Kerrn stopped with her hand just above the bag. 'You stole a jewel, just as you did last year, in Wellmet. The Lady Rowan sent me to bring you, and it, to the posting inn on the road to Wellmet. I must be certain that it is in here.'

I licked my lips; they were dry and chapped. 'It's in there, Kerrn. If you touch it, it'll kill you.'

She studied me for a few moments, her eyes cold. 'Very well,' she said at last. Carefully, she picked up the bag by its string and held it above her saddlebag. 'Will it be safe in here?' she asked.

I nodded.

Kerrn opened the saddlebag and dropped the leather bag inside. Then she picked up my knife from where I'd lost it during our fight, put it in the pocket of her robe, and swung up onto the horse. In the saddle, she unhooked one of her canteens and took a long drink. 'You are thirsty?' she asked.

I nodded, suddenly tireder and hungrier and thirstier than I'd ever been in my entire life.

Kerrn held up the canteen. 'I know you, thief. You are trouble. Give me any problems and I will keep you dry. Understand?'

I nodded.

She leaned over to hand me the canteen and I drank deeply. The water went into me like rain onto dry ground – I soaked it in. 'Thanks.'

Kerrn frowned down at me. 'We are not far from the canyon lands.' The orange rocky place, she meant. She hung the canteen from her saddle. 'We will walk as long as we can before camping for the night.'

'I'll walk, you mean,' I said as I rewrapped my head scarf, awkward with bound hands. 'Me and the horse.'

Kerrn nudged her horse into a walk. Pulled by the tether, I fell into step behind them.

We walked in silence under the bleached-blue sky. *Plod, plod, plod,* toward the road to the posting inn, and to Rowan. Or, more likely, I realized, to Jaggus's trackers. He wouldn't let me, or his locus stone, go that easily. We needed to be going in the other direction, *away* from Desh. I'd have to watch for a chance to steal the jewel back from Kerrn and make an escape.

But not right now. I was too tired.

Right about when I didn't think I could take another step, we stopped, and camped for the night.

The next morning, Kerrn scanned the sky. The clouds over the mountains had come closer and looked heavy with rain.

Kerrn frowned at the clouds. 'We must move fast,' she said, tying my tether to the horse's saddle. 'We need to get through the canyon lands before the rains.'

We reached the canyon lands by mid-morning.

The clouds hung grey and threatening over our heads.

Even though I'd slept all night, I was already tired, tripping over my own feet, and hungry — we'd only had a little dried fruit for breakfast. The bird flapped from one perching spot to the next along our trail.

Kerrn reined her horse to a stop. 'We must move faster,' she said, looking down at me.

I pulled down my head scarf. 'I don't think I can go any faster.'

She stretched a hand down to me. 'You can get up behind. But do not try to escape.'

Without answering, I grasped her hand, put my foot atop hers in the stirrup, and let her pull me onto the horse's back. It sidled, but Kerrn patted its neck and spoke calmly, and it settled. We set off again at a faster pace.

The twisted orange rocks around us glowed in the gloom-grey light. The horse picked its way through ravines and switchbacks, Kerrn's hands steady on the reins. The clouds grew lower and darker; at last, the wind picked up and drops of rain splatted onto the dusty ground. Kerrn nudged the horse into a faster walk. We were nearly at the end of the canyon lands. The rain, icy cold, fell more heavily, until it was coming down in sheets. I shivered and held on to Kerrn's robe so I wouldn't slide off the back of the horse.

We came to the dangerous place, where the road edged along the rock face that sloped down to a steep cliff. Kerrn guided the horse onto the narrower trail.

We were halfway across when the storm's first burst of thunder and lightning struck nearby, a blast of light and ear-pounding sound that sent the horse whinnying and rearing with fright. I fell off at the first buck, flat on my back on the hard road, my hands still tied by the tether to the horse's saddle. Kerrn hung on for a moment longer, and then went flying, landing with a thump on sloping rock made slick by running water. She slid down, toward the edge of the cliff.

The horse shied to the side, dragging me with it; I scrambled to my feet and grabbed its reins, patting its neck as Kerrn had done to calm it. The horse stilled, but its flanks twitched as if it was still frightened. I was frightened, too; my heart pounded and my knees were shaking.

Rain slammed down all around us. I peered through the curtain of water, looking for Kerrn. At the very edge, far below, where the slope ended in the cliff, she clung to the rock face, her feet dangling over empty space. Pebbles and rain-water rattled down the slope past her, but she didn't move.

Because if she moved, I realized, she'd go over. Right.

I'd been waiting for a chance to escape; now I could take the horse and get away. I bent and pulled my other knife from my boot and used it to cut the ropes tying my hands. I took up the horse's reins and got ready to climb on. Then I took a deep breath and leaned my forehead against the saddle.

Raindrops poured down on my shoulders and on my head. The horse stood still, waiting.

Drats. If I left Kerrn, she would slide off the cliff and die on the sharp rocks below. I couldn't do it.

There was plenty of rope in the saddlebag. I tied one end tightly around the saddlehorn; then I knotted the other around my ankle. The horse stood steady as I got down on my knees and then flat on my stomach and crawled onto the slope, staying off to the side of where Kerrn had slid to a stop below.

The face of the rock was seamless and slick with rainwater. I slithered downward. My hair hung in wet rattails in my eyes. Pebbles I knocked loose rattled by Kerrn and fell down into the ravine, but she didn't move.

The rope was a little too short; I'd reached the end of it, the knot tight around my ankle, and I was still an arm's length above her.

'Kerrn,' I croaked.

She didn't look up.

'Captain Kerrn,' I said again, louder.

Moving in tiny increments, she tilted her head up, face pressed against the rock, peering through the pelting rain. Maybe she hadn't heard me coming, the rain was so loud. Her eyes widened. Slowly, she moved her hand higher up the rock face.

Beneath her, a few pebbles shifted, and she slipped a hair closer to the edge. She stilled, and her fingers whitened with the strain of clinging to the rock. She closed her eyes. The rain began to ease up; I heard a flash flood racing through the ravine below us.

I stretched as far as I could reach. 'Kerrn, take my hand.'

She didn't move, but she opened her eyes again. If she reached up, she'd just about be able to touch my fingertips.

'There isn't enough rope,' I said.

'I can see that,' she answered through gritted teeth.

'It's tied to my ankle,' I said. 'You'll have to grab my hand and then climb over me.'

'I cannot move, or I will go over.'

'If you don't move, you're going to go over anyway,' I said.

She tilted her head up a little more, and focused on my hand. 'How did you get your hands free?'

I half laughed. 'I had another knife, all right? Will you just reach out and take my hand?'

She took a breath to answer, and started to slide.

'Kerrn, hold on!' I shouted.

With a desperate lunge she flung herself toward my hand; I grasped her wrist tightly and grabbed her other hand. 'Go!' I gasped.

Without hesitating, she climbed over my back, careful where she put her feet, and used the taut rope to pull herself up the rock face. I got myself turned around and pulled myself up to the top, where I sprawled next to Kerrn in a mud puddle, panting and soaking wet, and covered with scrapes and scratches. Beside us, the horse was quivering, but held its ground. The black bird perched on the saddlehorn, shaking water off its feathers. A few drops of rain pattered down around us, and the sound of rushing water echoed from the ravine.

Kerrn got to her feet. Her white robe was covered with orange mud; her head scarf hung over one shoulder and trailed on the ground, and her unravelling blonde braid hung over her other shoulder. She gave me a curt nod; I figured she meant 'thanks.'

I grinned and sat up, and started to work on the rope knotted to my ankle. I wondered if she'd let me have the horse so I could make better time. I'd be able to outrun trackers with a horse. Or maybe she'd want to come with me. We could send a letter back to Rowan, telling her that we couldn't go near Desh with the locus stone, that we'd gone on to another city.

Kerrn went to the horse and untied the rope from the saddle. She pulled the knife from her belt and used it to slice off a new length of rope.

I looked up at her, swiping the wet hair out of my eyes, and held out my booted foot. The water had made the knot swell, and I couldn't get it off. Without speaking, she cut it from my ankle. Then she offered her hand. I took it, and she pulled me to my feet.

And she didn't let go of my hand. Before I could pull away, she looped the new piece of rope around my wrist, grabbed my other hand, and tied off the rope. 'Where is the knife?' she asked.

I stared at her. She wasn't going to let me go?

'The knife?' she prompted.

I didn't answer.

She pushed me up against the rock wall and searched me. When she found the knife in my boot, she glared at me. '*My* knife,' she said. Right, the one I'd nicked from her on the road. With the knife, she cut another length of rope for a new tether and tied one end to my hands, the other

to the saddle. She picked up the horse's reins and
led it along the muddy trail, and I stumbled along
behind her.

CHAPTER 30

After camping, we travelled most of the next day, me keeping my eyes open for trackers. We waited out the afternoon storm in a hut at Frogtown, sitting on the packed dirt floor while rain poured down outside. Kerrn sat cross-legged, inspecting the hem of her robe.

The light was dim; I didn't think she could see much.

I sat with my back against one of the mud walls, looking up at the ceiling, which was made of cactus ribs and dried palm leaves woven together. The rain falling on the roof made a pattering sound, like thousands of rushing feet. The bird stood in the doorway, looking out at the rain. My stomach growled.

I leaned my forehead against my bound hands. Explaining all of this in my next letter to Nevery was going to be tricky. And when we got to the posting inn, *if* we got there, Rowan was going to be very unhappy with me.

I looked out the open door, past the bird. While we'd been talking, the storm had eased off; the silver-grey curtain of rain opened to reveal the desert beyond the village, sparkling with raindrops which gleamed golden in the setting sun.

Kerrn hefted the saddlebags and, holding the end of my tether, headed out into the golden light, pulling me with her. Waiting for us was an old lady wrapped in rags and shawls.

'She caught you, did she?' the water-crone asked me.

As an answer, I held up my bound hands. The bird flew up and landed on my shoulder, gripping me with its clawed feet while it folded its wings.

Kerrn scowled down at the crone. 'You said he did not go that way.' She nodded toward the road we'd come in on. 'And I paid you five coppers for that information.'

The water-crone darted to the side and thrust something into my hands. 'Frogs is good luck!' she said, and then scuttled away, into one of the mud huts.

I opened the package she'd given me – palm leaves wrapped around flat bread, olives, and rancid white cheese. My empty, hollow pit of a stomach told me to bite off a chunk of the bread. 'Want some?' I asked Kerrn, my mouth full, offering the package.

She didn't answer, instead stalking across the village square to the horse. I followed at the end of the tether, splashing through puddles and eating green olives off a string. Not as good as Benet's biscuits, but enough to satisfy the hunger that had been gnawing away at me with little sharp teeth ever since I'd left Desh. I held up a chunk of bread for the bird to peck at.

Kerrn mounted up and nudged the horse into a walk; munching the last of the bread and cheese, I followed. I guessed we were going to walk through the night to make up the time we'd lost to the rains.

Frogtown was on a crossroads. We were just starting onto the road that led around Desh, toward the posting inn, when three men riding horses galloped up to us.

Krrrrr, the bird said in my ear.

The men were dark shapes against the setting sun. As they got closer, reining in their horses, I saw that they wore the uniform of the sorcerer-king's guard.

Their horses stood, blocking our way down the road. 'What do you want?' Kerrn said, putting her hand on the hilt of her sword.

The leader held up his hand. His four fingers were short, as if they'd been sliced off at the first knuckle. 'I am Half-finger, captain of my lord Jaggus's guard.' He nodded at me. 'I am sent for that one. And the jewel he carries.'

Kerrn stared down at me, frowning. I stared back at her. If she cut the rope tying my hands, I could help her fight them off.

Half-finger nudged his horse closer. He leaned forward. 'Our lord merely wishes to speak to him and then will return him to his friends.'

My heart started pounding. The guard was lying; Jaggus didn't just want to *talk* to me. I'd stolen his locus stone. He'd want to squash me, like he'd squashed the little lizard. 'Kerrn, don't let them take me,' I said.

The two other guards nudged their horses so they were behind Kerrn, surrounding her.

Kerrn glanced at them, then back at me. She nodded.

With one hand, she tore off her head scarf so she could see; with the other, she pulled out her sword and swung it round at Half-finger's head.

The bird flew up, off my shoulder. I ducked to get out of the way, but I couldn't duck too far because my tether was tied to Kerrn's saddle. From overhead, I heard the *clang-clang* of sword on sword and a shout from Half-finger. Kerrn's blade swept down and cut the tether rope.

I crouched down and grabbed up a double handful of sand, spun around to find a target, and threw it at one of the guards. He shouted and swung his blade at me. I ducked behind Kerrn's horse to get away, and it shifted sideways, knocking me over. From down on the sand, I looked up and saw a guard, a dark shadow against the orange sky, pull something from his boot, then lean forward and plunge it into Kerrn's back.

Kerrn's breath huffed out, and she tipped off her horse, falling like a sack full of stones down onto the sand beside me; her sword fell next to my head. I scrambled up onto my knees, going for Kerrn's sword, but Half-finger reached down from his horse and grabbed the back of my robe, jerking me away. I fell down onto my back on the rocks and sand, and Half-finger lowered the point of his sword until it hung before my face.

Catching my breath, I turned my head and saw Kerrn, lying a step away, staring back at me. Her breath gasped in and out, and her eyes were wide.

'Stand up,' Half-finger said.

Slowly I got to my feet, my hands still tied, the end of the tether trailing in the dust. I looked around for the bird, but didn't see it. Half-finger cut a new length of rope and tethered me to his own saddle.

The other guard reached over to Kerrn's horse and rummaged in the saddlebag until he found the bag with the locus stone in it. He held it up by the drawstring to show his captain, who nodded. Half-finger kicked his horse into a walk.

I looked back over my shoulder.

In the growing darkness, Kerrn lay on her back in the middle of the road. As I watched, the bird circled down and landed on the ground next to her. Then the tether jerked, and the sorcerer-king's men took me away.

CHAPTER 31

Stumbling after Half-finger and his two men, I looked down the road. It led toward the mountains where the sun had just set. The sky darkened to purple. 'What's down this

road?' I asked at last.

'The sorcerer-king's fortress,' Half-finger said.

His *fortress*?

I gulped down a lump of sudden fright. I darted forward a few steps and, with my bound hands, seized Half-finger's half-fingered hand where he held the reins. 'Don't take me there,' I said.

He shook me off. 'Be quiet.'

Overhead, the sky darkened; the night air was suddenly chilly, and I shivered. I'd have to try to escape and get to Rowan – even if it meant leaving the locus magicalicus.

'Please,' I said, leaning on his arm again.

This time, when he shook me off, I brushed my tied hands against his uniform and nicked his knife right off his sash, sliding it up the sleeve of my shirt, inside my robe. I slowed down until I was at the end of my tether again. We walked for a while in silence. Half-finger glanced over his shoulder at me; in the growing darkness, I doubted he could see much. His two men rode silently beside him.

When he looked away again, I slid the knife down to my hands. Holding it between my palms, I bent my head – hoping he wouldn't turn around – and, taking the handle of the knife in my teeth, sawed at the rope. The guard captain kept his knives sharp. Slice, twice, and my hands were free. I held on to the end of the tether and looked up. Half-finger and his men faced forward, noticing nothing.

Taking a deep breath, I dropped the end of the tether, whirled, and tripped over a stone. Drats! I scrambled to my feet and started running. Behind me, a guard shouted.

At that very moment, the moon popped up over the horizon; the road before me lit up like a river of milk. I ran on, looking for a side trail, but all I saw was a swirl of shadows and thorny bushes. If I could hide and then get back to Frogtown, maybe the water-crone would help me. Kerrn might be all right and we could make our way to the posting inn together. I raced onward – then something grabbed my foot and I went sprawling, landing hard on the rocky road. I rolled over and reached down, touched rope, and went for the knife to cut it. Horse hoofs crunched over the road, and another loop of rope dropped over my arms, then cinched tight.

I looked up and caught my breath. Each one of the guards held the end of a rope. Between them, Half-finger, bathed in moonlight, looked like a statue made of slowsilver.

'Drop the knife onto the ground,' he said. 'And then stand up and move away from it.'

I thought about it, then did as he ordered.

He dismounted and, keeping his eyes on me, picked up the knife. 'Turn around.'

Slowly, I turned around. Was he going to stab me in the back, like one of his guards had done to Kerrn? I hunched my shoulders.

'Put your hands behind your back,' Half-finger said.

I did it, and he tied them, the rope burning where it rubbed against the raw skin of my wrists. I kept quiet. At least he hadn't stuck the knife in me.

He dropped another loop of rope around my neck, but let it lie noose-loose. Then he went back to his horse, tied the new tether to the saddle, and mounted. He pointed to the road. 'You walk ahead.'

I walked ahead. Leading them toward the sorcerer-king's fortress.

We walked for a long time, the moon tracking high above us in the purple-black sky. Once we stopped and Half-finger watered the horses, but he didn't give me any water. I swallowed down dust and stood quietly, with my head down, trying to think. Jaggus wanted me brought to his fortress. Why? To kill me?

And why did he have a fortress outside Desh? His power came from the magic, and the magic was in the city, not out here in the desert. It didn't make sense.

I thought about Kerrn, back at the crossroads. The knife had gone into her back, but she was still breathing when they'd taken me away. She might be all right after a while, and she had her horse, and the bird. She might be able to get to the posting inn and tell Rowan what had happened. But even if she did, what could Rowan do about it? She was angry with me; she might not want to do anything. She might go back to Wellmet without me.

Half-finger and the guards mounted up again and waited for me to start walking, then nudged their horses into a walk, following.

On we plodded, through the night. I walked slowly, and even the horses looked tired, hanging their heads.

Something was ahead, I could feel it in my bones. It wasn't magic, I didn't think, because it felt heavy, like dread, or a nest of a thousand misery eels. As we went on, the feeling grew stronger, like it was pulling me in.

Finally the sky lightened to grey – and stayed grey, because storm clouds hung low over our heads. The feeling of dread faded as the sky grew lighter.

I stumbled and looked ahead, down the road.

The fortress. It was built of polished white stone, with high walls all around the outside, square towers on each of five corners, and one tall, thin tower in the middle, like a bony white finger pointing at the sky. As we came closer, a ray of sunlight broke out of the clouds and glinted off the tower, and it glittered white, like old, polished bones.

The dread feeling had come from the fortress. I stopped in the middle of the road. Half-finger didn't say anything; he and the guards just rode past me until the rope around my neck tightened and I had to stumble along after them.

We came up to the high walls, which were so thick the gateway was a dark and clammy tunnel. We passed through that and into a courtyard.

It was empty. Ahead was the fortress, a huge block built of white stone, with narrow slits for windows and a huge front door, shut tight and banded with metal.

Behind us, back down the tunnel through the

wall, another door closed with a clanging boom, and I heard the rattle of chains and locks.

Half-finger climbed down off his horse. He held my neck-noose tether, so when he started walking I had to follow him in a side door, across a wide, white, dusty hall, and up some twisty stairs. We went up and up, into one of the towers, I guessed. Was Jaggus up there, waiting for me? My heart pounded, and I panted, trying to keep up with him.

He stopped at a doorway just off the stairs and jerked me closer to him with the tether. Then he took out his knife. Before I could squirm away, he used the knife to cut the rope from my neck, and the one from my hands. Then he opened the door and shoved me inside.

The door slammed and locked behind me, a puzzle lock from the sound of it, with a trick-barrelled key and double-click flange.

I took a deep breath and looked around.

Dear Nevery, I thought as I examined the room.

I've gone to stay at Jaggus's fortress for a while. The room was big – maybe fifteen paces across – and empty, except for dust, and made of white stone. The air was cold and dry. It was dim – the only light came from the narrow slit of a high window. I went and jumped and caught the edge of the window with my fingers; I pulled myself up, resting my chin on the stone sill to look out. The walls were thicker than my arm, so I could only see a narrow slice of desert and, in the distance, mountains. I dropped to the floor again, raising a little cloud of dust. *My room has a good view*, I added to the letter in my head. I examined the smooth, white walls. *And the stonework is very fine*.

I slid down the wall and sat on the dusty floor. My bones ached with tiredness. I leaned my head back against the wall and closed my eyes. They weren't going to kill me, at least not right away. If that had been the plan, they would've done it right after they'd taken me from Kerrn. So they were saving me for something else.

I slid farther down, to lie with my back against the wall. Even though I was worried about what Jaggus planned for me, I was too tired to stay awake. My eyes fell closed and I went to sleep.

When I woke up later, the room was dark and I heard the lock turn over. The door swung open and a gust of dusty air blew into the room. I creaked to my feet and leaned against the wall. Half-finger came in, carrying a lantern that burned with sickly green werelight and a tray with bread and a jug of water on it. In the darkened doorway lurked a Shadow, watching me with its glowing eye.

'Take off all your clothes,' Half-finger said, 'and put these on.' He tossed a shirt and trousers onto the floor. A little cloud of dust puffed up and settled.

I looked at the clothes, then up at Half-finger and shook my head.

He took a half step forward. The green were-light flared. 'If you don't do it yourself,' he said softly, 'I will have this one help you.' He nodded at the Shadow behind him.

No, I didn't want that kind of help. I pulled the sand robe over my head and dropped it on the floor.

'Show me your hands,' Half-finger said.

I raised my hands, which were empty.

He nodded and watched very carefully as I stripped off the rest of my dirty, smelly clothes and my boots, and put on the ones he'd brought in. They were too big. I rolled up the sleeves of the shirt and cinched the drawstring belt on the trousers, but they still hung loose.

I bent over to pick up my old clothes.

'Stop,' Half-finger said; he put his hand on the hilt of his sword. 'Back away.'

I straightened and did as he'd ordered. The Shadow stayed in the doorway, watching.

Half-finger went to my pile of clothes and nudged it with his foot, then bent and picked up my shirt. It was ragged and filthy. It took him only a moment to find the lockpick wires sewn into the collar. He nodded to himself and scooped up the rest of my clothes and boots, and carried them out of the room. The Shadow flowed after him. The door slammed behind them and locked.

Drats. *They're taking very good care of me, Nevery,* I added. *I won't be leaving here anytime soon.*

CHAPTER 32

The bread was hard as rocks, but after soaking it in the water, I ate and drank. I was tired enough after that to go to sleep, but first I had to try to get out.

I tried the door. The lock was impossible without lockpick wires. The hinges were on the other side, so I wouldn't be able to work on them, either.

Then I tried the window. The walls were as thick as I was tall, and the window was just a narrow slot. If I lay sideways, I might be able to squeeze far enough out to see what was what. Maybe the wall outside would have some nice cracks in it; maybe I could climb down and get away. I jumped up and caught the windowsill and pulled myself up. I squeezed myself in on my side, wriggling forward. Outside, I heard the *hiss, hiss* of wind blowing past the tower.

I wriggled farther into the window slot until I put my chin over the rough edge of stone and looked down. The wall was slick and smooth, just like inside. And it was way too far to jump. I wriggled back out again and dropped to the floor of my cell.

Drats. I was stuck.

I lay down with my back against the wall to sleep. My eyes were just closing when I heard a fluttering at the slitted window.

A bird sat there, folding its wings and fixing me with a sharp, yellow eye.

'Hello,' I said, sitting up. My voice sounded thin in the empty room.

Awk, said the bird.

'D'you have a letter for me?' I asked.

It did. It swooped down from the window to the floor and let me take the roll of paper from the quill tied to its leg. A letter from Nevery.

Connwaer,

It has been ten days since your last letter. I must conclude that either you have broken your promise to report your progress, or that you have gotten yourself into some sort of trouble in Desh and cannot write. Your previous letter leads me to believe that Jaggus has something to do with it. I trust that the Lady Rowan is safe; she, at least, knows how to look after herself.

When you have received this, write at once.

– Nevery

I had nothing to write with, but Nevery was going to be furious if he didn't hear back from me. I looked over his letter again.

I did have something to write with, of course. Carefully, I tore a few scraps from the paper, scraps with words written on them. With my teeth, I ripped the edge of my sleeve, then picked free a rough thread and bit it off. I took the paper scraps that read *Rowan is safe* and tore *cannot* in half for *not* and *in Desh*, rolled them together, and tied them with a length of thread. Then I put together another message – *Connwaer* and *into some sort of trouble* and *Jaggus has something to do with it* – and tied it with another bit of thread. Both the notes I slid into the quill tied to the bird's leg.

'Off you go,' I said. Nevery would know what the notes read; and he'd have no difficulty believing I'd gotten myself into trouble. I wasn't sure what he could do about it, though.

The black bird flapped up to the wide window-sill and perched there, then it hopped forward and launched itself out into the grey day.

I hoped it would hurry. Then I went to sleep.

I woke up when I heard the *jink-clink-kajink* of the key slotting in and the puzzle lock turning over, and then the door swung open.

'*Lothfalas,*' said a voice with a sharp accent, and the room filled with brilliant light.

I blinked the brights from my eyes. Jaggus stepped in, holding his locus magicalicus. He had a big, furry lump on his shoulder. Half-finger stood in the doorway behind him, and in the hallway outside, I saw Shadows flinching away from the light.

'Ah, here you are,' Jaggus said. 'My black shadow.'

I wasn't *his*. I got to my feet and leaned against the wall and didn't say anything. Maybe he'd tell me why he'd brought me here.

'Bring me my chair,' he said without taking his eyes off me. Behind him, Half-finger nodded at somebody. After a moment a chair appeared; the guard captain set it inside the room, then stepped back to fill the doorway.

Jaggus settled himself on the chair. The light from the locus stone stayed bright, filling the room with sharp shadows. The lump on his shoulder turned its head and I saw that it was a white cat with a flat face, sharp, raked-back ears, keen pink eyes, and a long white tail.

'My Shadows have been watching you for a long time,' he said. 'I know who you are, Connwaer. Not a servant of the Lady Rowan, but a spy and thief. I venture so far as to guess that you are the young wizard responsible for the disruption of our plans last year in Wellmet.'

Our plans? 'What d'you mean?' I asked.

'You had not realized?' He smiled. 'The wizard Pettivox and the Underlord Crowe. They did not know the role they played, but they served our purpose. We supplied them with slowsilver and with the plans for their device. They were weakening the magic of Wellmet, making it ready for me. And they would have succeeded if not for you.'

I shook my head, trying to get the new thought into my brain. Crowe and Pettivox, and their device. That had all been part of *another* plan – Jaggus's plan? 'Why?' I asked. 'I mean, why did you attack Wellmet's magic?'

'I can think of a better question,' Jaggus said. His long, thin fingers stroked his locus magicalicus, which looked like a clot of blood in his hand. 'Why were you brought here, my shadow? That question will exercise your clever brain, will it not?'

That question was already exercising my brain; I didn't need Jaggus to ask it.

'Well, I will tell you,' Jaggus said. 'I did not bring you here. *It* did.'

It?

On his shoulder, the white cat watched me with sharp eyes. Jaggus gave a small, secret smile. 'Arhionvar brought you,' he said.

I stared at him. What was he saying?

'You understand, don't you, little black shadow?' he said. 'Arhionvar is a magic, just like the magic of your city. Arhionvar is here. It has chosen you, just as it chose me.'

Oh. The dread I'd felt outside the fortress. It was a magical being, he was saying. But magic without a city? That was wrong. It couldn't be right. I didn't understand, no matter what Jaggus said.

'Now, because Arhionvar wants you,' Jaggus said, 'we will help you. To begin with, we will help you find another locus magicalicus.'

Another locus stone? I straightened up from the wall and stared at him.

Jaggus smiled. 'Ah, I see that this interests you.'

It did.

'Pyrotechnics is your current method, I believe, as you have no locus stone. I will give you slow-silver. And tourmalifine, and whatever other materials you need. You may use my workroom. I will teach you a finding spell, and you can use

325

pyrotechnics to cast it.'

A finding spell? That was a very good idea. I didn't know any finding spells; I wondered if Nevery did.

'We will find your locus stone. Wouldn't that be nice? And then you can join us.'

I shook my head. Finding my locus stone would be more than nice. But I wasn't going to join Jaggus and his dread magic.

Jaggus frowned. 'Well, then.' On his shoulder, the white cat yawned, showing off long, sharp teeth. 'I will give you a night to think about it. Arhionvar will persuade you.' He got to his feet. 'Have a pleasant night, my little shadow.'

Taking the bright locus light with him, Jaggus and the guard captain left the room. The door swung closed and locked.

By the time they left, I was so tired my thoughts were whirling around inside my head.

So was the spellword the Wellmet magic had

spoken to me.

Damrodellodesseldeshellarhionvarliardenliesh.

The dread magic's name was Arhionvar. *Arhionvar.* Another part of the spellword. The magic of Wellmet had known about the dread magic all along. *This* was why it'd sent me to Desh. I was supposed to deal with Arhionvar.

I fell asleep thinking about magical beings without cities and finding spells and Jaggus's strange cat.

I woke up in the blackest, darkest part of the night. The dark pushed up against my eyes.

Something was in the room with me. I could feel it, pressing down on me like cold stone until my breath came short. I sat up and backed into a corner and opened my eyes wide, straining against the dark, trying to see. Misery eels? I waited for the soft, icy touch of a misery eel on the back of my neck. Nothing happened; they didn't come.

The air grew heavier, and the feeling of dread gathered in my stomach and spread outward into my arms and legs and up into my head until all I could think of was dread. I heard my own breath, gasping in and out, and behind it the roar of the room's quiet. Was there a Shadow in the room with me?

No, not a Shadow. It was Arhionvar.

I curled into a ball in the corner for a long time, my eyes squeezed shut and my teeth clenched to keep from crying out loud. The dread magic watched me, and it waited. I felt like I'd been turned to stone.

Slowly, the watching dread went away, like a heavy hand being lifted from the top of my head. After a while, I caught my breath and stopped trembling, and sat up against the wall. The long slit of a window had turned grey – morning had come.

CHAPTER 33

In the dusty, grey light of morning, I heard the key in the lock and got to my feet.

It was Jaggus and his cat. He looked me over with a keen eye. 'A bad night?' he asked.

I shrugged.

'Were you persuaded?' he asked.

I shook my head. No.

Jaggus ordered his chair again and sat down. He held his locus magicalicus in his hand. In the dim room it looked dull and dark. Darker than before, I thought, as if the rot in its centre had spread. It meant Jaggus was rotting too, weak and ready to crumble. 'A fine jewel,' Jaggus said. 'Just as your locus magicalicus was.'

I nodded. Except that my stone hadn't had a poisoned, rotten centre.

'See?' Jaggus said. 'You and I are just alike.'

I blinked. 'No, we're not.'

'Try not to be stupid, shadow boy. We are the same. Let me prove it to you. I have received reports. Your Lady Rowan has left you behind and fled back to Wellmet. You have been exiled from your city by the very people who should be your colleagues and friends. Your own master has disavowed you. You are alone, are you not?'

I shrugged.

Jaggus frowned. 'Before you became a wizard. You were alone then, were you not? The most miserable, lonely person in your entire city?' He nodded. 'When Arhionvar came to Desh, the magic of the city was weak from years of slow-silver mining. Arhionvar knew it could take the city, but it needed a wizard to do its work in the world. It chose me above every other wizard in the city because my family sold me into the service of a master whom I hated. Your Wellmet magic chose you, shadow boy. Not because you were a great sorcerer, but because you are just like me. You are alone.'

While he spoke, my heart started pounding and I leaned back against the wall because my knees were shaking. He was right. Before I'd picked Nevery's pocket on the streets of the Twilight, I had been, sure as sure, the most alone person in all of Wellmet.

'And now your own magic has cast you out,'

Jaggus said. The darkness grew in his eyes, blotting out the blue, and his voice got deeper. 'You are alone again. But Arhionvar wishes to take you up. Join us, and you can be a sorcerer. You will not have to be alone anymore.'

I shook my head. 'Wellmet didn't cast me out. It sent me.'

'You are lying to yourself if you think so,' said Jaggus. 'You have no locus magicalicus. You are useless to your magic.'

I gulped down a sudden surge of fright. 'I won't join you, Jaggus,' I said.

He leaned forward, his eyes empty windows. 'I can see, my shadow,' Jaggus said, 'that you must think further on this. Arhionvar will visit you for another night or two. I will come back when you are persuaded.'

That second night alone in the dark was worse than the first. I was like a wet cloth, and the dread magic picked me up and wrung me out until I was dry, and then stretched me out and carefully tore me into rags. It got into my head and made me think of all the bad things that had ever happened to me. Exile from Wellmet, Heartsease a ruin, Benet hurt. Dee dead and cold. The cell full of misery eels under Pettivox's house. Nevery saying he didn't need an apprentice. Shivering in cold doorways with nothing to eat. Being led into a room with a bed in it and seeing Black Maggie, my mother, lying still and white and cold. Leaving me alone.

No. The bird was on its way to Nevery. I was *not* alone. I pushed away the rags and bits of memory and fixed my thoughts on the bird. The connwaer, a black shadow swooping over the golden, thorny desert. Then over the grasslands and through the dark forest, pausing to perch on a high branch to rest. Then on to Wellmet. It flapped up to a window at the academicos and went *tap-tap-tap* with its beak against the glass. The window cracked open and it hopped inside.

Morning came at last. I uncurled myself from my corner, stiff and aching in my bones. I didn't know if I could last another night like that one.

The day got later and later. I couldn't stop thinking about the dread magic. What would happen if I gave in and let it have me? I'd be like Jaggus, was what. My own dread grew and grew. I went to the door and checked it, but it was locked, and then I paced around the room and checked it again. Still locked. Curse Half-finger for taking my lockpick wires.

Night was coming.

I sat with my back to the wall with my arms wrapped around my knees, and watched the window slit. The sky outside, the narrow slice of it that I could see, grew darker, but it was too early for night. Then I heard a rumble of thunder, far away, and rain started. It came down hard, like a waterfall, and even in the high-up tower room I could smell the wet desert. The dry dust in the room settled.

At the window came a flap and flutter, and the

black bird tumbled in. It hopped to its feet and shook a spatter of rain off its wings. Then it flew down to the stone floor.

Its quill was longer this time. My hand shaking, I untied it carefully, turned it upside down, and tapped it. A roll of damp paper fell out, and also two wires bent in half – lockpick wires.

The letter was from Nevery, of course, but the rain had gotten into the quill, leaving the letter nothing but smudges. That was all right. I could guess what it said.

CHAPTER 34

I had the whole night before anyone would come looking for me. As soon as the sun set, I brought the lockpick wires over to the door. I'd heard the lock open and close enough times to know exactly what it looked like inside. *Quick*

hands, steady hands, I picked the lock. I eased the door open and peered out into the hallway. It was empty and dark. After slipping out the door, I slunk down the hallway, quick-quiet on my bare feet. Then down some stairs, across another hallway, and down again, until I got to the ground floor.

Nobody was about. I felt the heaviness of the dread magic gathering. I wondered if all the human guards hid themselves away at night when the magic came out. I wasn't sure about the Shadows, though.

My legs were shaking, and I couldn't quite catch my breath. Not enough to eat and not enough sleep. I stayed close to the walls in case I stumbled, and crept through empty stone rooms on the ground floor until I found a small doorway at the end of a passage that let out at the edge of the courtyard.

Every thief knows, when planning to steal something, that the first thing you do is find another way out of the place you're sneaking into. That way, if the job goes wrong, you may not nick the thing you came for, but at least you don't get caught at it.

Jaggus still had his locus magicalicus, and he and the dread magic were planning some kind of attack against the Wellmet magic. They must have tried weakening the Desh magic with slowsilver mining, just like they'd weakened the Wellmet magic with Crowe's prisoning device. I had to stop them if I could. But first I needed an escape route.

I opened the door onto the courtyard and looked out. The rain had cleared off, and the clouds had thinned enough that the moon, a little off full, shone through, making the night shadowy, not completely dark. A good night for creeping around.

I crept across the courtyard until I came to the wall, and then I followed it away from the main gate, hoping I'd find a smaller door, one less likely to be guarded. Sure enough, I found one, down at the end of a passageway through the thick wall.

The lock on the outside door was a simple lock. After picking it, I put the lockpick wires into my pocket and cracked the door open.

The door was jerked out of my hand and swung wide.

A shadow loomed up before me. 'Be still,' growled a deep voice, and then a cold sword edge rested against my neck.

I stayed still. Why did they have guards on the *outside*?

'Wait,' said Rowan's voice. 'Conn, is that you?'

I laughed. I'd thought she'd be halfway to Wellmet by now. 'Hello, Ro.'

Argent was the one holding the sword; it glinted in the faint moonlight. Rowan was just a shadow behind him. She pushed Argent's sword arm down, swept past him, and grabbed me into a fierce hug.

'You're all right?' she asked, letting me go.

I nodded.

'Don't *ever* do anything like that ever again, Connwaer,' she said.

Argent muscled in between us and grabbed me by the scruff of the neck. 'I should cut your throat right now,' he growled, 'for all the trouble you've caused.'

'He *has* caused us trouble,' Rowan said. 'But he came to meet us. That's something, Argent. Let him go, and we can be off.'

Argent let me go.

'Ro, did you bring the guards with you?' I asked.

Her face looked pale in the moonlight. 'Conn, we're all here. We've been searching for a way in for hours. But we didn't have anyone who could pick the lock on this door.' She gave me her slant-smiling look. 'We're leaving Desh, and we came this way because we guessed you might be imprisoned here. Come along.'

I shook my head. 'I can't.'

Argent growled. He still had his sword out. Kerrn stepped up beside him.

'Hello, Kerrn,' I said, glad to see her. 'You're all right?'

'I am well enough,' she said. 'No more talking; we must go.'

I stepped back into the doorway. 'I can't leave,' I told them.

They were silent, staring at me.

'You don't have to come,' I said quickly. 'But I have to find Jaggus and destroy his locus magicalicus, and if I can't do that, I have to steal it again.' That was the only way I could think of to deal with Arhionvar as the magic of Wellmet wanted me to. Without Jaggus and his locus magicalicus, Arhionvar wouldn't have a wizard to do things for it, like order the mining of slowsilver in Desh to destroy its magic or make Shadows to attack Wellmet.

More silence. Then, 'I suppose you have a

good reason to do this,' Rowan said, her voice shaking.

I nodded. 'The same reasons as before. You could wait out here. I'll try to hurry.' I thought of something. 'Can I borrow a sword?'

Kerrn huffed out a breath that sounded like a laugh. Then she winced. 'I will come with you, thief, if the Lady Rowan permits it.'

'All right,' I said. 'Let's go.' I felt the dread magic swirling around. We needed to hurry.

'We'll all come,' Rowan said firmly.

'What is the guard contingent?' Kerrn asked.

I thought back. 'At least three guards, and one of them is Half-finger, the captain. There might be more that I didn't see. And some Shadows, I'm not sure how many. We have to get past them to get to Jaggus.' I decided not to tell them about Arhionvar; it would take too long to explain.

Argent went to bring up the guards. Rowan stepped up next to me and handed me a sheathed sword on a belt; she wore her own sword at her waist.

'Would Magister Nevery approve of what you're doing, Conn?' Rowan asked quietly.

She didn't know about the birds or my letters from Nevery. 'He would, Ro, sure as sure,' I said. My stomach growled. 'D'you have anything to eat?'

She gave a half laugh. Kerrn gave her something, and she passed it along to me. A bag with food in it, cheese in a roll of bread. I took a big bite. She held out her canteen. I took it and had a long drink. Much better.

I heard the *shuff, shuff* of footsteps on sand, and Argent came up with seven guards. He'd left three with Nimble, he said, who refused to come along.

'You lead,' Kerrn said.

I gulped down the last of the roll and cheese and hung my sword belt over my shoulder. 'Be as quiet as you can,' I said, and led them back into the fortress.

The guards wouldn't have made good thieves because their footsteps echoed on the stone floors and they kept whispering questions to each other, and to Kerrn.

Jaggus, I guessed, would have his workroom in the tall tower in the middle of the fortress. It would likely have only one door in, and if any guards were around they would be there.

We rattled around the ground floor rooms for a bit, like noisy shadows, until we found a wide staircase leading up. A lone werelight turned low glowed from the top of the stairs. I headed toward it.

I got to the top step and paused; the guards and Rowan and Argent waited on the stairs behind me. At the top of the stairs was a wide landing. The werelight lantern hung from a hook beside a door, casting a small circle of greenish, wavery light onto the floor. Everything else was dark.

The door led to Jaggus's workroom, sure as sure. He couldn't have left it unguarded. It'd be locked, anyway. I felt in my pocket for my lock-pick wires.

'Wait here,' I said over my shoulder.

Leaving Rowan, Kerrn, Argent, and the guards at the top of the stairs, I bare-footed across the landing to the door.

I crouched down to have a look at the lock, putting my sheathed sword on the floor next to me. Taking out a wire, I probed inside to see what I was dealing with. *Steady hands*, and then a faint, oily click.

Drats. Quickly I pulled out the wire. A fret-lock. It had a set mechanism inside, and if I tripped it, the lock would realign itself and I'd have to start over again. This would take some time.

I glanced back toward the stairs. I couldn't see the others. Outside my circle of greenish light, shadows flowed. A finger of clammy, dusty air stroked across the back of my neck. '*Shadows!*' I whispered. I caught a glimpse of a purple-black eye and boiling black shadows.

I heard the sound of bootsteps rushing up the stairs and the hiss of a blade being drawn from a sheath. 'On your guard!' Kerrn shouted.

I shoved the lockpicks into my pocket, grabbed up my sword from the floor, and leaped to my feet. Three Shadows gathered at the edge of the light, reaching toward me with long tendrils of darkness.

I fell back against the door and wrestled the sword out of the sheath and swung it one-handed round at the Shadows. The blade sliced through one of them, and it dissolved into black rags of shadow that swirled, then re-formed around the pulsing eye.

From the stairs, I heard more footsteps rushing up, and shouting – Half-finger and his men had snuck up on the others from behind. Another werelight flared. In the faint greenish light, the landing was full of swooping Shadows, and a swarm of fortress guards with swords, fighting with the Wellmet guards.

'Conn!' Rowan shouted. She was in the middle of the fighting. Her sword flashed in the dim light as she parried a thrust by a fortress guard. With her other hand, she reached out and yanked his head scarf over his eyes, then reversed her sword and clubbed him across the back of the head. He crumpled to the floor. Another fortress guard lunged at her and she whirled to catch his blade on her blade.

Yet another guard attacked her, and Argent leaped to her side, his blade slashing across the man's chest, spattering the floor with blood. The guard groaned and fell backward. Two more fortress guards attacked them.

I couldn't hide in my bit of light while Rowan and Argent did all the fighting.

With a quick lunge, like Kerrn had taught me, I poked my sword into one of the Shadows.

The blade went right in, then I pulled it out with a *pop*. Dust crumbled along the sharp edge. The Shadow swooped down on me again, and this time, when I swung the blade around, it sliced through its darkness, hitting the darksilver eye with a *clang* that vibrated up my arm. The Shadow exploded into black dust, and darksilver rained down around me, burning where it touched my skin.

Brushing off the steaming drops of darksilver, my bare feet sliding over dust, I stepped out of the circle of light, heading for Rowan and Argent, where the fighting was thickest. They stood back-to-back, their swords flashing, defending themselves from three fortress guards.

Keep your guard up, I told myself. I gripped my sword and plunged into the fight. A guard swung his blade at me, and I ducked out of the way and swiped back at him, but missed. Rowan caught my eye and nodded, then said something over her shoulder to Argent, who glanced my way.

A swathe of shadow reached from behind me and tightened around my neck. I spun around, slashing with my sword, but it cut right through the shadows. The numb-stone feeling spread. I gasped for breath. Then a sword plunged past me and straight into the Shadow's staring eye.

The Shadow blew apart into a cloud of dust, releasing me.

I whirled back and caught Argent's nod as he brought his blade back around to block a thrust from a fortress guard.

Another guard came at me, his blade feinting and glinting in the dim light. I flailed out with my sword, just missing Argent. 'Careful!' he shouted, blocking my wild swing.

'Sorry,' I gasped.

The fortress guard came at me again. I ducked to the side, and then somehow his blade cut around, slashing toward my head.

I brought my own blade up in a desperate parry. The guard ducked as I swung wide; then my sword slipped from my grip, spinning round until its tip sliced across my arm, right below the elbow, tearing a ragged gash through the cloth of my shirt. The sword clattered to the stone floor and spun away. I scrambled after it, ducking another blow from the fortress guard.

'Get out of the way!' Argent shouted, doing some fancy footwork to keep from tripping over me.

He was right; I wasn't any use to them. I needed to get back to the door. I grabbed up my sword and tried to get my bearings.

'Conn!' Rowan shouted. She kept her eye on two Shadows, hovering just out of reach of her blade.

'Here!' I answered, from behind her.

She spun around and grabbed my arm, right where my own blade had cut me. Ow. It hadn't hurt right away, but I could feel it now, a nasty gash cutting deep into the muscle.

'To the door!' She dragged me away from

the fighting and over to the circle of light by the door. 'Do what you have to do,' she ordered, and let me go. Her hand came away covered with blood. She looked at her hand, then at me, with wide eyes.

'I'm all right,' I said, and went to crouch by the door. I dropped my sword onto the floor and pulled out my lockpick wires.

I closed my eyes, feeling my way into the fret-lock. The sharp end of the wire brushed over the set mechanism. Two tumble-bolts, I thought, and a spring-set puzzle ratchet, and in front of it, the fretwork. Right.

Closing my ears to the sounds of fighting, I took the other wire from my mouth and probed into the lock, listening for the snick of the set. There. *Steady hands*, and I flicked the other wire into place.

An oily click, and the lock reset itself. *Curse it!*

'Hurry!' Rowan said from behind me.

'Ro, I need you to hold this,' I said.

I heard a swish of cloth, and she was crouched beside me. 'What?' she said.

I took the wires out of the lock and steadied my hands to try again. 'Hold the wire when I say,' I said.

She nodded.

Careful, careful, past the fretwork and bolts and ratchet. Then the second wire.

'All right, hold it,' I said.

Rowan reached out and held the end of the wire. Her hand stayed absolutely steady.

I probed the fretlock. Then a quick twist and a double flick, the lock turned smoothly over, and I was in. I glanced aside at Rowan. 'You'd make a good lockpick,' I said. She gave me a quick grin and leaped to her feet.

My ears opened again to the sound of fighting, and I glanced back over my shoulder.

Half-finger and a Shadow were headed for Rowan.

'Can you hold them?' I asked.

'Go!' Rowan shouted, and brought her blade up.

I grabbed up my sword and leaped through the doorway, slamming the door behind me.

CHAPTER 35

The stairway was completely dark. With the door closed, the sounds of fighting were muffled.

I had to hurry. Rowan and the rest were out-numbered, and if Jaggus brought the dread magic to bear on them, they wouldn't last long.

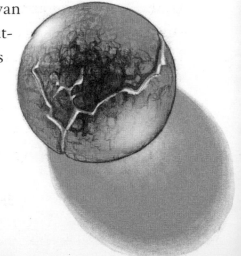

My bare feet silent on the stone steps, I raced upward. The stairs twisted round and round, higher and higher. My legs grew tired and my breath tore at my lungs. Blood from the gash dripped down my arm.

As I climbed, the dread magic grew thicker in the air, pressing down on me. Arhionvar knew I was coming. I took deep breaths and made myself go faster, *step, step, step* through the darkness.

The door at the top of the staircase was open; white-bright light blazed from the doorway. I slowed down, catching my breath, waiting for my eyes to adjust. The air was thick with the dread magic; it made every breath heavy; it made my bones shaky. I'd gotten this far, and now I wasn't sure what I was going to do. Still, I climbed up the last two steps and stood in the doorway.

The room was at the very top of the tower; it was clean and full of sharp-edged shadows, and set in each of the four walls was a tall, wide-silled, open window looking out at darkness. White-bright flames flickered along the edges of the ceiling and floor, and light blazed from Jaggus's locus magicalicus, which rested in a dish full of sparking darksilver in the middle of a high table. Three white cats lay on the table around the dish. Jaggus himself sat on a stool, staring into the locus stone, carrying another cat on his shoulders. I wondered what he was looking for.

'Ah, Connwaer,' Jaggus said. 'We knew you would come back to us.' He turned slowly to face me. The pupils of his eyes were huge and blank-dark, like the windows.

The dread magic was in his head, clear as clear. Was it looking out at me through his eyes? Did it make his thoughts heavy and numb?

'Are you going to attack us?' Jaggus asked.

I'd forgotten I was holding the sword. Slowly I bent and put it on the floor. As I straightened, drops of blood from the gash in my arm spattered onto the white stone; the blood looked black in the bright light. 'I don't want to fight you, Jaggus,' I said.

And I didn't. He was right. He and I *were* just alike. We'd both been alone. I wasn't alone anymore, not with Nevery and Benet and Rowan for friends. But Jaggus was alone except for Arhionvar in his head all the time, *using* him, and his loneliness. Now I understood his true name. No wonder he was broken.

'You did not come to attack us?' Jaggus said.

'No,' I said. 'I'm not a guardsman, I'm a thief. I came to steal your locus magicalicus.' On the table, the stone rested in the sparking dish of darksilver. It was darker than before; the poisoned part in its centre had grown. It was nothing but rot.

'To steal it?' Jaggus pushed away the cats and picked up the dish, holding it with the tips of his fingers, as if it burned. Darksilver smoked and sizzled all around the locus stone. Even from where I stood, I could see how deeply rotted it was. 'You cannot steal my locus magicalicus. If you hold it in your hand, Arhionvar will take you, and you will be ours. Here it is.' He held out the dish.

I took a deep breath and stepped forward.

Slowly I raised my hand and reached into the dish and picked up the sorcerer-king's locus magicalicus.

Like a thick, black wave, Arhionvar surged through the stone and into me. I gasped for breath as it wrapped around me, prying with fingers like knives into the darkest corners of my head. It was far stronger coming through the stone than it had been when I was alone in my cell.

'You will belong to it, just as I do,' Jaggus whispered. His eyes were wide and dark.

The dread magic howled around me. I struggled, and it squeezed tighter. Pain slashed into me, blazing into my bones. Darkness came with the pain, pressing down on me heavier and heavier with dark dread. Arhionvar had attacked Jaggus the same way once, and Jaggus had let it take him.

With every scrap of strength that I had, I pushed the magic away. '*No!*' I cried out loud.

As I pushed, the darkness all around me became the fluttering of black-feathered wings. It became the black yarn of the sweater Benet had knitted me, and the black silk dress Rowan had been wearing the first time I'd met her. It was Nevery's black eyes, glaring sternly at me. *Get on with it, boy*, he said.

Right.

I opened my eyes.

Jaggus stood staring at me. 'We knew you could not resist. Now you will join us.'

'No,' I said sadly. 'You are going to join *me*.'

I was a wizard with no locus magicalicus. And Jaggus would be, too. I held up the red jewel stone. I could see the soft, slimy rot at its centre. I didn't need to be a wizard to do this. I closed my hand and squeezed as hard as I could. With a muffled *pop*, the locus stone burst apart like an overripe plum, then turned to dust in my hand.

Jaggus stared at me, his mouth wide, then stared at the dust falling to the white floor. The black windows in his eyes snapped shut, he blinked, and his eyes turned blue. The cat leaped from his shoulder and dropped to the floor. 'No,' he whispered.

He fell onto his knees and, using his hands, started sweeping up the dust that had been his locus stone. *'No, no, no, no,'* he said. He scrabbled up two hands full of dust. It leaked out between his fingers.

He looked up at me. His braids had loosened and hung in his face like white cat tails; his blue eyes were wide and streaked with blood. 'Arhionvar!' he screamed.

The words echoed against the white walls. The magic couldn't hear him, not without a locus stone. I knew how he felt; I'd lost a locus stone once, too.

'Don't leave me,' Jaggus moaned. He climbed to his feet.

Then he whirled and staggered across the room to one of the tall windows and stepped up onto its wide sill.

I knew what he was going to do, to prove his tie to the magic. But Jaggus was nothing to Arhionvar now.

'No!' I shouted, starting after him.

'Arhionvar!' Jaggus shouted, and he stepped out of the window.

I flung myself after him, flat down on the sill, reaching down with my hand.

I caught him. His hand was like a claw. 'Hold on!' I gasped.

He stared up at me, his eyes wide. Blood from my arm dripped down onto his face.

'Don't let go,' I said.

'Let me go,' he whispered. 'Arhionvar will not let me fall.' He jerked himself upward and dragged his fingernails along the gash in my arm. His hand slipped out of mine.

Jaggus hung in the air for a moment; he stared up at me, and his laugh was a high, scared sound. Arhionvar held him, and then it let him go. Jaggus's laugh turned into a scream. Down he fell, turning over and over like a leaf in the wind, until the blackness swallowed him up. He was gone.

Rowan Forestal

Argent and I fought the remaining fortress guards and the Shadows to a standstill, and then we raced up the winding stairs of the tower to the room at the top. We found Conn there, hanging half out of one of the room's windows.

I feared that he was dead, he was so still and pale.

We wrapped him in a blanket, and Argent carried him out of the fortress. We found Nimble, Kerrn brought up the rest of the guards, and we fled across the desert.

I looked back at the fortress. The desert sand blew around it, and I saw Jaggus's guards fleeing it, on horseback and on foot. The wind whirled, sucking up sand until the fortress was hidden by a huge, swirling vortex of sand and wind and black clouds.

We didn't stay to watch any further.

When we arrived at the crossroads, I had Nimble take a look at Conn, who was still unconscious.

Soon after, Conn woke up long enough to drink a little water and mutter something about Arhionvar, and then he fell asleep.

He slept in the wagon until we reached the posting inn. When he awoke, I asked him how he had defeated the sorcerer-king. He looked unhappy and said, I didn't. He defeated himself. He refused to say any more about it. Then he asked for something to eat. I assume this means he will be all right.

CHAPTER 36

At the posting inn, I woke up long enough to eat and to write a long letter, which I sent off with a connwaer.

Dear Nevery,

We're all well. I've figured out what's going on.

Our magic knew all along that the trouble came from Desh. Nevery, I really didn't use that much explosive material when I blew up Heartsease. The magic was trying to tell me, and I didn't listen.

Our Wellmet magic is afraid, and it can't do anything but wait. It trusts us to help it. Our magic knows about the dread magic because the dread magic helped Pettivox and Crowe with the prisoning device, and it sent the Shadows as spies to see if our magic had gotten weaker and as attackers to make the Wellmet people weaker, and more afraid. I don't know what it wants to do. Maybe kill our magic, but I don't know why.

The dread magic is terrible, Nevery. Its name is Arhionvar. We have to stop it.

I am coming home soon. Please tell Benet that if he makes biscuits, I will eat every last one.
— Conn

We passed slowly from the posting inn through the grasslands and into the forest, the days getting colder and the nights even colder than that. Rowan had brought my black sweater with her from Desh, and she found me new boots and socks at the posting inn, so I was all right, though as we got closer to Wellmet I wished for a coat.

As I walked along at the back of the envoyage, I thought about what had happened in Jaggus's fortress. I wondered if the Wellmet magic really had chosen me because I'd been alone. I had a feeling Jaggus had been wrong about a lot of things, but he was right about that. He knew what it was like to be completely alone. He'd said his family had sold him into service. His master must have been very cruel for him to turn to Arhionvar instead. I had Nevery and Benet and Rowan and Wellmet's magic protecting me; he had been alone and empty, and his magic had poisoned him. I wished I could've helped him.

During our travels, Kerrn watched me like a hawk watches a mouse. She gave me and Rowan and Argent swordcraft lessons. I still got the fluff beaten out of me every time, and Rowan teased me about dropping my sword in the middle of the fortress fight and about almost cutting my own arm off.

She'd ended up that night with a sword cut across her cheek, and it scabbed over and left her with a pink line of a scar.

I knew we were getting close. The rain started up. I walked along at the back, but I wasn't plodding or thinking bad thoughts about the rain. From ahead, I felt the magic of Wellmet. When I'd left, it had wanted me to go so much that it had pushed me down the hill and made the bird scoff at me. But now it pulled at me, wanting me to hurry home.

I looked up. At the top of the hill, ahead, I saw where the road led into Wellmet, and on the buildings alongside the road perched hundreds of black birds, all rustling like leaves in a breeze. More birds flew in wide circles overhead, calling *awk, awk*.

Ahead of me, the envoyage headed off the dirt road and onto the cobbled street, into the city, but Kerrn got down off her horse and stood at the side of the road, waiting for me to catch up.

I grinned at her – I was glad to be home and couldn't help it.

The birds perched on the houses grew still, watching. I was just about to step into the city, when Kerrn stepped in front of me and put her hand on my chest. 'If you take another step, I will arrest you.'

I stared at Kerrn. Her face was blank.

'Did you expect anything else?' she said. 'You are exiled.'

Oh. The same way I was a wizard, Kerrn was a guard captain. Of course she had to do this.

I heard the sound of hooves clattering on

cobbles, then Rowan rode up and stopped. She leaned over to speak to us. 'Captain Kerrn, what's going on here?'

Kerrn's face stayed still, like stone. 'Lady Rowan, it is my duty to enforce the laws of the city. This boy' – she pointed at me – 'is under an order of exile. If he sets foot into the city, he will have broken the law, which means I must arrest him.'

Rowan straightened in her saddle and gave Kerrn her best commanding look. 'Captain Kerrn, you know this is ridiculous. It is only thanks to Conn that we were able to deal with the sorcerer-king, and we need him to help prepare the city for a possible magical attack.'

Kerrn didn't answer; she didn't even glance up at Rowan. She lowered her hand from my chest. My choice, then.

I stared right back at her. Then I lifted my foot and stepped forward, into the city.

CHAPTER 37

In the guardroom at the Dawn Palace, Kerrn and her guards searched every stitch of my clothes, from my boots to my black sweater. They even checked my hair.

They found my lockpick wires and a knife. Then they gave me back my clothes and boots and marched me down to one of the prison cells under the palace. As we went down the steps, the air got heavier and colder, and smelled of old stone. They shoved me into a cell and slammed the door. The keys turned in the lock, a heavy plunger with two flanges, from the sound of it.

I'd picked that lock before. I could pick it again if I had the tools. The cell was the same one Kerrn had put me in after I'd stolen my locus magicalicus from the duchess's necklace. It was cold and shadow-dark; the only light came in through a barred window that opened on an air shaft. A table and chair were pushed up against one of the stone walls, which had patches of dripping mould on it.

Drats. I'd been spending too much time lately locked into places I needed to get out of. I had to talk to Nevery. Arhionvar was done with Jaggus. It had filled up his emptiness and aloneness with poison, and then it had tossed him aside. It needed a new wizard now, and it wanted me for that. Arhionvar was done with Desh, too, and it would be coming for Wellmet, now that the magic was weakened and the people afraid. We had to get ready to defend the city.

Cold seeped from the damp walls and into my bones, making me shiver. To keep warm, I paced the room, five steps across, five steps back. Would Nevery come? Maybe he didn't want to see me. Somewhere in the palace, up above, Rowan was arguing with her mother about the order of exile. I hoped she would win the argument, but I didn't think she would.

Hours passed.

I was tired, but I couldn't sleep.

At the sound of keys jingling in the lock, I whirled to face the door. It creaked open, and a dark shadow stepped into the doorway. The shadow spoke a word, and a locus magicalicus burst into flame.

I ducked my head away from the light.

'Well, boy?'

I blinked the brights out of my eyes and saw

that the shadow was Nevery, stepping into the cell and looking around, frowning. Kerrn stood behind him in the doorway, her face blank.

'Very well, Nevery,' I said. Now that he was here.

'Hmph. I see you've gotten yourself into trouble again.'

Not *again*. This was my old trouble, just working itself out to its end. 'I had to come back,' I said. 'Wellmet's magic's in danger.'

He stared at me, pulling on the end of his beard. 'Yes. I received your letter.'

'Can you get me out of here?' I asked. Could he get the order of exile taken back, is what I meant.

'No,' he said.

Oh.

Nevery reached into his bag and pulled out a bundle of cloth, which he held out to me.

Before I could reach out to take it, Kerrn stepped out of the doorway. 'What is that?' she demanded.

Nevery scowled. 'You put my apprentice into this freezing cell, Captain. I brought him a coat so he won't be cold.' He held out another packet. 'And biscuits,' he said to me, 'from Benet.'

'He's all right?' I asked.

'He is,' Nevery said.

'I will examine those things,' Kerrn said.

'Very well,' Nevery said.

Kerrn opened the packet of biscuits and broke them open. She shook the coat and checked the pockets. Then she handed the coat back to Nevery and put the biscuits on the table.

Nevery held out the coat again, and I took it.

He turned to leave.

'Nevery—' I took a step after him, then stopped myself from trying to follow him out.

He turned back and put his hand on my shoulder; I leaned my head against his arm and took a deep, shuddery breath.

'All right, my lad,' Nevery said, his voice rough. For a moment he rested his other hand on the top of my head. Then he let me go and turned away again, and left the cell.

Kerrn, looking unhappy, followed him out.

After the door slammed closed and the keys jingled in the lock, I unfolded the coat. Nevery must've gotten it from a used clothes shop. It was black, with a shabby black velvet collar, and it smelled a little mouldy. I put it on and rolled up the sleeves.

No, Nevery had said. He wasn't going to try to get me out, then. I shivered and huddled into the coat.

No, wait. I was being stupid. I knew Nevery. He wouldn't leave me locked up in here.

I took off the coat again. I felt along the sleeve seams. Nothing. Then in the hem. Nothing. The buttons were ordinary buttons. There was nothing hidden in the lining. Then I found it, a slit at the edge of the shabby velvet collar. I poked around with my fingers, and then I found them.

I pulled them out, two long, thin wires.

Thank you, Nevery.

Nevery was a wizard, but he knew how to think like a thief.

He'd brought me lockpicks.

A GUIDE TO
PEOPLE AND PLACES

PEOPLE

ARGENT – A noble young man with a sense of honour but no liking for former thieves and gutterboys. He is an expert swordcrafter and has been giving lessons to Rowan, but lately she's been improving and might even be better than he is.

BENET – A rather scary-looking guy but one who loves to knit, bake, and clean. His nose has been broken so many times, it's been flattened. If he were an animal he'd be a big bear. His hair is brown and sticks out on his head like spikes. You wouldn't want to meet him in a dark alley, but you would want to eat his biscuits.

CONNWAER – Has shaggy black hair that hangs down over his bright blue eyes. He's been a gutterboy for most of his life, so he's watchful and a little wary; at the same time, he's completely pragmatic and truthful. He's thin, but he's sturdy and strong, too. He has a quirky smile (hence his quirked tail as a cat). Conn does not know his own age; it could be anywhere from twelve to fourteen. A great friend to have, but be careful that you don't have anything valuable in your pockets in reach of his sticky fingers.

DEE – A gutterboy, he is thin and dressed in rags. He has blond hair and watery blue eyes and his front teeth stick out. He never gets enough to eat. He sneaks and spies for the Underlord's minions; one day, if he grows big and strong enough, he will become a minion himself.

EMBRE – A young man about eighteen years old. He is very thin and has a sharp face with dark eyes and black hair, and he might have smudges on his hands and face from working with black powder. Everything about him is sharp, including his intellect.

JAGGUS – The sorcerer-king of the desert city of Desh. He is young but has white hair that he wears in cat-tail braids all over his head. His eyes are blue; he likes to wear white clothes with gold and silver embroidery on them. He keeps cats as pets. He has a sad history.

KERRN – The captain of the Dawn Palace guards, Kerrn is tall and athletic; she wears her blonde hair in a braid that hangs down her back and has sharp, ice-blue eyes. She is an expert swordfighter. She speaks with a strong accent because she comes from Helva, far away from the Peninsular Duchies.

NEVERY FLINGLAS – Is tall with grey hair, a long grey beard, shaggy grey eyebrows, and sharp black eyes. He's impatient and grumpy and often hasty, but beneath that his heart is kind (he would never admit it). Mysterious and possibly dangerous, Nevery is a difficult wizard to read but a good one to know.

ROWAN FORESTAL – A tall, slender girl of around fifteen, with red hair and grey eyes. She is very intelligent with a good, if dry, sense of humour. She is the daughter of the Duchess of Wellmet. She is also very interested in studying swordcraft.

PLACES

ACADEMICOS – Set on an island in the river that runs between the Twilight and the Sunrise, the academicos is a school for the rich students and potential wizards of Wellmet. Conn enrolls there after becoming Nevery's apprentice.

DAWN PALACE – The home of the Duchess and Rowan. The palace itself is a huge, rectangular building – not very architecturally interesting, but with lots of decorations crusted on it to make it fancy.

HEARTSEASE – Nevery's ancestral island home. The middle of the house was blown up by Nevery's pyrotechnic experiments twenty years before this story. So the two ends of the house are left standing and the middle looks like it has a bite taken out.

MAGISTERS HALL – Seat of power for the wizards who control and guard the magic of Wellmet. It is a big, imposing grey stone building on an island with a wall built all the way around it at the waterline.

JAGGUS'S FORTRESS – The sorcerer-king's secret fortress is built of bone-white stone and stands alone in the middle of the desert.

WELLMET RUNIC ALPHABET

In Wellmet, some people write using runes to stand for the letters of the alphabet. In fact, you may find some messages written in runes in *The Magic Thief: Lost*.

a	l	tt
b	ll	u
bb	m	v
c	mm	w
d	n	x
dd	nn	y
e	o	z
ee	oo	
f	p	
ff	pp	
g	q	
gg	r	
h	rr	
i	s	
j	ss	
k	t	

Uppercase letters are made by adding an extra line under a letter; for instance:

Uppercase A

Uppercase B

RUNIC PUNCTUATION:

Beginning of a sentence ·
End of a sentence (full stop) :
Comma ℮
Question Mark ℈

BENET'S CHICKEN POT PIE WITH BISCUIT CRUST

4 tablespoons butter
½ cup flour
2 cups chicken broth
1½ cups milk
Chicken, cooked, cut into cubes
½ teaspoon nutmeg
A little lemon juice
A little white pepper

Melt butter in pan. Add flour, stirring. Remove from heat, add chicken broth. Stir. Add milk. Stir over low heat until simmering. Remove from heat and whisk vigorously until smooth; return to medium heat for one minute. Turn off heat, mix in chicken, nutmeg, and lemon juice and white pepper to taste.

Next:
2 tablespoons butter
1 chopped medium onion
1½ cups chopped carrots
¼ cup chopped celery
¾ cup peas
3 tablespoons fresh parsley, chopped

Melt butter in pan. Cook vegetables until soft. Add vegetables to chicken mixture. Put in baking pan. Preheat oven to 200°C. Add biscuit crust; bake.

BENET'S BISCUIT CRUST

1 recipe biscuit dough:
2 cups all-purpose flour
½ teaspoon salt
4 teaspoons bee's wing (baking powder)
2 teaspoons sugar
½ cup butter
½ cup milk

Mix dry ingredients together in bowl. Cut in butter until fine and crumbly. Make a well in these ingredients and pour in milk. Knead with your fingers only until blended—do not over-work or dough will be hard and flat. Roll to one knuckle thick. Cut and lay out biscuit dough in squares on top of chicken and vegetable mix. Brush top with beaten egg to make it brown during baking (not required). Bake at 200°C for 25 to 30 minutes.

CONN'S FROG POT PIE WITH BISCUIT CRUST

A lot of butter
Two handfuls of flour
About two cups of milk
Lots of pepper

Melt butter in pot. Add flour and milk and mix up really well with a spoon.

Frogs, cooked
Whatever kinds of vegetables you can find.
Potatoes and carrots and beans are best.
Also turnips.
Chop them with a knife and cook them with butter.
Mix frogs and sauce and vegetables.
Put in pot.
Make biscuits. Put on top of pot.
Bake in a hot oven until it is done.

SOME NOTES ON SWORDCRAFT
BY ROWAN FORESTAL

(learned from Kerrn, captain of the Dawn Palace guards)

Swordcrafting is the art of fighting with the sword.

Though swordcrafting is an art, it is not for duelling and not for show. It is for fighting. If you are not prepared to fight, then you should not take up swordcrafting.

The four elements of swordcrafting are distance, perception, timing, and technique.

Quickness can defeat strength.

Cleverness can defeat strength.

Strategy is one thing. Tactics are something else.

 ## SOME TERMS

EIGHTS High parries.

KEEP YOUR GUARD UP The sword is a defensive weapon as well as an offensive one; every defensive move and every offensive move comes from a basic position of readiness.

PARRY A defensive move; a block; moving your opponent's blade aside with your own. *Three notes on parries:* One, parry with the flat of the blade, not the edge. Two, parry to deflect your opponent's blade, not chop it in half. Three, the best parry is the beginning of an attack (see *riposte*).

PELL A training post made of wood; a target.

QUARTERS Low parries.

RIPOSTE An attack made immediately after a parry.

SALLE A training room.

STOP-THRUST An attack made into the opponent's forward motion.

WASTER A wooden practice weapon; a practice sword.

THANKS TO...

My editors, Antonia Markiet and Melanie Donovan, and my agent, Caitlin Blasdell. And the HarperCollins team: publisher Susan Katz, associate editor Greg Ferguson, associate editor Alyson Day, editorial director Phoebe Yeh, copy editor Kathryn Silsand, designer Sasha Illingworth, artist Antonio Javier Caparo, publicist Cindy Hamilton, sales reps (the ones I've met so far) John Zeck, Sue Farr, and Rick Starke.

To my first readers and dear friends: Jenn Reese, Heather Shaw, Greg van Eekhout, Steph Burgis, and Chance Morrison.

To my twin, Sandra McDonald. And to Haddayr Copley-Woods.

To the Dragons of the Corn, the best critique group in eastern Iowa: Lisa Bradley, Rachel Swirsky, Cassie Krahe, and Deb Coates.

To the Blue Heaven crew: Charlie Finlay, Bill Shunn, Paolo Bacigalupi, Holly McDowell, Heather Shaw, Rae Dawn Carson, Toby Buckell, Paul Melko, Ian Tregillis. But I don't thank the tick.

To Maud and Theo.

Most of all, to John, the best husband in the world, and still a very decent critiquer.